Hagar Lyndon

Hagar Lyndon

Or, A Woman's Rebellion

Lizzie Holmes

Introduction by

Michelle M. Campbell

Hastings College Press | Hastings, Nebraska

Introduction © 2019 by Hastings College Press

Text © 1893 by *Lucifer the Light-Bearer*. This book has fallen into the public domain and is no longer subject to copyright protection.

Production Staff

James Clapham	Taylor Lipinski
Dany Cook	Milli May
Davianne Czarnick	Daniel Trevithick
Kaitlin Grode	

ISBN-10: 1942885679
ISBN-13: 978-1-942885-67-2

Note on the text: This edition has been reset from the first (1893) edition. Original spelling and grammatical conventions have been maintained, except in the case of publishing errors in the first edition. The original punctuation has been maintained but updated using modern conventions (e.g., eliminating spaces around dashes).

Manufactured in the United States of America.

Contents

Appendices

HAGAR LYNDON;
Or, A WOMAN'S REBELLION.

BY MAY HUNTLEY.

CHAPTER I.

"THE SANCTITY OF THE HOME."

"Long ages gone she laid
Under the ban
In Eden's garden made
Subject to man.
Now as the dawning light greets her sad eyes
Comes the awakening thought 'Might I not rise?'"

A little, common place village stood on the banks of a pretty stream in one of the middle states; a village which contained the usual "post-office, store and blacksmith shop," two or three rival churches, one principal street and several small cross streets; whose inhabitants were of the ordinary village type—people strongly addicted to old customs and habits, with set opinions, deep prejudices and tendencies toward intense condemnation of all things wicked.

Toward one end of the principal street stood a plain brown cottage, the home of James Lyndon. The house contained his wife and six children also, but these were of no particular importance in the community. Mr. Lyndon himself, though but an overseer in a flouring mill, was a greatly respected citizen, a deacon in his church, one of the town trustees, a model before all the younger men, of stern and strict integrity. No one exactly loved him, but that did not matter, respect and deference are better than affection to some men. He was always at his post, wherever that might be: on Sunday three times at church; during working hours, frowning and giving orders somewhere in the mill; in the evenings, he could ever be found in the "bosom of his family." Mr. Lyndon possessed all the virtues—and yet contributed as little happiness to the human race in general as a man well could and live. No word of complaint ever passed the lips of wife or children; but her sad, white face, and their cowed wistful looks told a silent story of their own.

One evening, in the fall of the year, the father and four children were seated at the supper table. Mrs. Lyndon was still attending to something on the stove, carrying a baby on one hip while she hastily worked with the free hand.

"Martha!" called out the husband and father in a stern voice. "You know I will not have this fussing about when you have once said the meal is ready. Sit down."

"Yes directly—I only wanted a moment"—and she sat down nervously with inward misgiving as to spoons and salt and the insufficient steeping of the tea.

"Where is Lucy?"

Mrs. Lyndon looked up deprecatingly. "I had to send her to the store for a few little things for breakfast. I think I heard her come in the back way a minute ago—she is probably cleaning her rubbers and will be in in a moment."

Mr. Lyndon scowled. "A very shiftless, loose way of doing things. You should think of everything you will need when you order your groceries, and never send a child out for a "few little things" so near night. Never let it happen again. We will wait just two minutes for her."

Two minutes of absolute, dreary silence ensued. The potatoes steamed away their heat and the meat plate cooled while the hungry children looked longingly at the vanishing vapors. Then the father angrily bowed his head and pronounced a vindictive sounding "grace." The meal proceeded in silence. Mrs. Lyndon's face grew paler and more anxious

moonless night was settling down; a cool wind rattled the the crisp, fading leaves of trees and shrubbery and the few street lamps seemed to burn dimly in a discouraged sort of way. A lane crossed the street on which the Lyndon's lived not far from their gate. At the corner, a great beech tree with low hanging branches grew and cast a shadow beneath that was always heavy. Toward this Mr. Lyndon hurried. A moment before a woman's form well wrapt up had glided swiftly up from the other direction; he did not see it, but as he was about to go on, he heard a low voice in the shadow.

"Lucy, go quickly—run to the back door—your father—" the rest was lost. Then came an unintelligible word in a man's voice.

"The devil!" this pious man ejaculated as he made a dash into the darkness. He caught a young man by the collar and gave him a fling without looking to see where he landed; grasped a young girl by the shoulders, gave her a terrific shaking then pushed her in front of him until they reached his own door when, opening it, he flung her inside. The slight woman with her head wrapt in a shawl followed, trembling and silent.

"I'll teach you to disobey me you young hussy! I told never to speak to that wicked scamp again. You are forbidden to be out of the house after dark, and here I find you hiding behind a tree in the night with the worst rascal in town. I'll cure you, Miss."

He reached up for a long slender black whip which hung on the wall.

Lucy, a well grown girl scarcely fifteen had picked herself up and stood facing him. Her sullen defiant face with its flashing black eyes and flaming cheeks possessed the sort of beauty that aggravated her father. He liked to see women quiet, meek and colorless—that brilliant, dashing look, too early matured, he considered in itself a crying sin and ought to be whipt out of the girl. He gave her a fierce blow across the shoulders.

"James!" cried the mother piteously. "Don't! I'm sure she will never disobey you again. Oh don't whip her—that will never cure her—leave her to me, I'll talk to her."

"You, madam! You are scarcely fit to speak to your children much less teach them. A woman who will lie to her husband to screen his children in their wrong doing, who will encourage them in disgracing themselves, needs disciplining herself. Badness runs in your family. Your daughters, if they depended on your guidance alone, would follow in the footsteps of your wicked, fallen sister, and God knows what you would have been if I hadn't married you and kept you straight."

A momentary fire crept into the weary eyes. "James, do you insult me before our children? You know our family is a most honorable one, and never knew disgrace until poor Clive so unfortunately trusted—"

"Silence woman! How dare you answer me back? I'll attend to your case presently."

He turned toward his daughter again and raised the whip.

"James! You must not! Think of it. Our first born, almost a woman, to strike her like a brute—" she laid a beseeching hand on his arm. He struck it off and gave her a violent push. The poor woman's short lived daring deserted her; she caught herself from falling, took up her baby and bent her tearful face low over its soft and tender one. There was nothing more she could do—the mother heart must bleed in vain, while a heavy hand rained blows on her beloved first born. What she had so dreaded was passing now and she could do nothing. Ah! you who write so beautifully of romantic sorrows and picture human woe in scenes of

Introduction

Michelle M. Campbell

Hagar Lyndon was serialized under the pen name May Huntley in 22 issues of the periodical *Lucifer the Light-Bearer* from March 1893 to September 1893. This edition is the first time the novel has been published in its entirety and the first time it has been accessible to the general public since its original publication. Compiled from microfilm archives at the Kansas State Historical Society, this edition recovers an important radical literary work of the nineteenth-century Midwest and is one part of a larger effort by scholars to recover and piece together a history of forgotten women writers and anarchist writers of the nineteenth century. Indeed, *Hagar Lyndon* is a crucial text for anyone studying nineteenth-century American social issues, women's writing, radical literature, or the U.S. Midwest.

The protagonist of Lizzie May Swank Holmes's radical 1893 novel *Hagar Lyndon; Or, A Woman's Rebellion* is a woman far ahead of her time. After watching her mother die in childbirth and her sister forced into an emotionally and physically abusive marriage as a teenager, Hagar Lyndon, a young woman from a small, repressive Midwestern town, decides she does not want to marry. She does want to be a mother, however. Simultaneous acceptance and rejection of traditional gender roles forms the central dramatic conflict of the novel, as Hagar is willing to risk all to avoid the same fate as her mother and sister. Though the novel contains biting critiques of the church, state, love, marriage, and small-town life in the Midwest, Hagar Lyndon learns that freedom comes at a cost and tradition is a vicious beast to slay.

Tracing Lizzie May Swank Holmes

Less is known about Lizzie May Swank Holmes than about other radical women of her time, such as Emma Goldman or Lucy

Parsons, but what little is known reveals her investment in late nineteenth-century radical and anarchist politics. In the only scholarship devoted solely to Holmes and her writing, "Free Love and Domesticity: Lizzie M. Holmes, *Hagar Lyndon* (1893), and the Anarchist-Feminist Imagination," Blaine McKinley traces Holmes's journey from rural Ohio to burgeoning Chicago, where "she became involved in the fledgling Working Women's Assembly 1789 of the Knights of Labor in the early 1880s" (55). McKinley contends that, after her marriage to English-born William Holmes, Holmes and Lucy Parsons "form[ed] the nucleus of Chicago's English-speaking anarchist movement," and Lizzie Holmes "led a parade of 300 or 400 women through Chicago's streets demanding the eight-hour day" on May 3, 1886—only a day before the Haymarket bombing (55). Holmes was the assistant editor of the Chicago-based anarchist periodical *The Alarm* and was arrested alongside Parsons during the Haymarket Affair, though both were later released without being charged (Marsh 108). In a 1907 piece in the Duluth, Minnesota *The Labor World*, Holmes told the reporter,

> In middle life I became well acquainted with several
> of the brainiest, ablest, most devoted men I had ever
> seen. For three years I went to their meetings, heard
> their speeches, and listened to their conversations. I
> knew and felt to my innermost being how their hearts
> burned within them for the wrongs done to working
> people, how they yearned to do something to free
> them, and how their whole beings were absorbed in
> the great cause of the freedom of the workers. ("Let
> No Man" 1).

After the Haymarket Affair, according to James Green in *Death in the Haymarket*, Holmes and her husband left Chicago and moved to Denver, and, as the *fin de siècle* neared, she doubted her anarchist ideals would soon come to fruition (299). Green explains, "Holmes admitted that the anarchists buried as Waldheim no longer had a known following and that their lives and their ideas no longer held deep meaning for working people" (299). Even still, Holmes remembered the Haymarket Martyrs fondly, even if she was pessimistic about their ability to bring the revolution. Holmes's 1899 contribution to *Free Society,* titled "Revolutionists," reflects on the men, many of whom she knew personally. Holmes explains that a revolutionist "sees a vision of society as it should be, thrown up against the sky of the future, and all his mighty energies are bent upon making it a reality. The terrors facing him do not count; the immediate perils are small compared to centuries of anguish stretching behind him, and the marvelous possibilities glowing in the future" (179). At the end of the article, she writes of the anarchist men hanged for Haymarket, "But—ah, let us never forget the men who could rise to heights we perhaps never could, or blame them for being the lofty souls they were. The martyrs of the race have been its saviors" (180).

Emancipating Women from Sex Slavery— *Hagar Lyndon* and *Lucifer the Light-Bearer*

From its genre to key themes to intertextual references to biopolitics, *Hagar Lyndon* is a complex text that is both literature and cultural artifact. For starters, *Hagar Lyndon* is a novel that follows in the genre of sentimental fiction. As many scholars like Jane Tompkins and Shirley Samuels have shown, sentimental fiction was a prominent mode of fiction writing in the nineteenth century, and it was a popular way to write, especially for women. Often, sentimentality was not considered as serious or literary as realism, which was the other popular genre for fiction in the late nineteenth and early twentieth centuries. The goal of realism, usually dominated by men, was to paint an often stark portrait of how things were, and realism was lifted up as the privileged literary mode. Classic novels such as or Frank Norris's *McTeague* (1899) or Theodore Dreiser's *Sister Carrie* (1900) are examples of literary realism that depict the lives of women similar to Holmes's Hagar, but in a very different way. In particular, the characters of Trina and Carrie are both intelligent young women eager to escape their class stations: Trina marries McTeague, an untrained dentist, and Carrie attaches herself to a series of men who promise her the wealth and excitement she craves. Trina's marriage to McTeague implodes after he loses his career, and she is a victim of domestic violence. Carrie, however, finds that men lead only to disappointment and leaves them behind in quick succession when her career as an actress takes off. Like Trina and Carrie, Hagar successfully escapes both her class station and the traditions of womanhood, namely marriage, that have entrapped her mother and sister. Among these three characters, Hagar is the only woman who actually gets it all, though: because of her rejection of marriage and her dedication to emancipated motherhood, she gains class station, individual freedom, and the love of the man whom she loves in return.

The goal of sentimentality was to evoke emotion from the reader, usually with the goal of changing hearts or minds. A well-known example of sentimental fiction is Harriet Beecher Stowe's anti-slavery novel *Uncle Tom's Cabin*, which is credited with helping to turn the tide toward the abolition of slavery. A more contemporaneous example is Frances Ellen Watkins Harper's recovered novel *Iola Leroy, or Shadows Uplifted* (1892), which is a retrospective text about a mixed-race woman during and after the U.S. Civil War. Like Holmes, Harper uses sentimental conventions to deal with very serious social problems and works to give readers an aspirational view of the future, even if it is only thinly sketched.

In the case of *Hagar Lyndon*, sentimentality is deployed as a device to evoke pity from the reader for Hagar's mother and sister, who are "slaves" of marriage and tradition. Additionally, sentimentality is used to cultivate sympathy for Hagar, who is a beautiful but strange child who grows into a woman with radical, but principled ideas of the role of women and marriage. Readers are supposed to identify with Hagar in order to fulfill the novel's didactic purpose: to teach women there is a way to be a successful mother and a successful lover without having to submit to the everyday horrors of servitude and "sex slavery" that marriage often entailed.

Anarchist feminists in the late nineteenth century often referred to the state of married women as "sex slavery." In the postbellum period, after black slaves were emancipated through the Civil War and resultant emancipation proclamation, feminist writers used abolitionist critiques of slavery and the language of emancipation as powerful rhetorical models to expose the plight of women. Although some economic opportunity existed in the late nineteenth century, women had to fight to be admitted to universities and professional education, and women were legally paid less than men. Economic emancipation, or the ability for a woman to support herself, was key in helping women to escape "sex slavery."

Lucifer the Light-Bearer was a consistent and significant supporter of women's emancipation in the latter decades of the nineteenth century. Based in Kansas and later Chicago, *Lucifer* was one of the many politically radical periodicals in the Midwest that published essays, poetry, editorials, commentary, and fiction of interest to anarchists, socialists, free lovers, spiritualists, and other radicals. *Lucifer the Light-Bearer* was first published in Valley Falls, Kansas, then in Topeka, Kansas, until finally moving, along with its editor Moses Harman, to Chicago, Illinois, in 1896. According to an advertisement in its own pages, "The Object, the Mission of LUCIFER, as the Etymology of the Word itself indicates, is to 'Spread the Light.' That is to say, its mission is to investigate, to discuss ALL Questions affecting Human Welfare. To show that the popular prejudice against the name 'Lucifer' is a false and misleading one we quote from Webster's Unabridged Dictionary: 'Lucifer [Lat. Light-bringing, the morning star, from luz, lueis, light, and *ferre*, to bring.']" (February 7, 1890).

The publishing industry was not always an easy road for Moses Harman. In 1890 he was tried and convicted for violating the Comstock Law. According to Hal D. Sears, "The federal postal obscenity law of 1873, the Comstock Act" was "initiated through the efforts of vice-suppression societies and their knight errant, Anthony Comstock" (37). The Comstock Law drew serious concern from free thought and radical groups, and for good reason: "The law prohibited obscenity from the mails, without defining it" (Sears 37). Anarchist, feminist, free-lover, and spiritualist Lois Waisbrooker took over the publication of *Lucifer* while Harman was serving his sentence, but in 1892, Holmes's sister, Lillie D. White, took over publication due to Waisbrooker's failing health. Holmes's mother and brother also contributed to the periodical in which *Hagar Lyndon* was serialized (Sears 245).

In an 1895 essay entitled "Sex Slavery," Voltairine de Cleyre, Lizzie Holmes's contemporary and an anarchist from Michigan, supports *Lucifer*'s vision. Critical of the jailing of Moses Harman for violating the Comstock Law, she takes up the cause of women's emancipation. De Cleyre explains that Harman, "beheld every

LUCIFER---THE LIGHT-BEARER

VALLEY FALLS, KANSAS, JAN. 17, 290.

M. HARMAN, Editor and Publisher.

OUR PLATFORM.

Perfect Freedom of Thought and Action for every individual within the limits of his own personality.

Self-Government the only true Government. Liberty and Responsibility the only Basis of Morality.

Second Indictment Defense Fund.

Previously acknowledged	$553.35
C. Trumbull Hayden, Tempe, Arizona,	1.00
Sallie Davis Hayden, " "	1.00

Sexual Science Educational Fund.

Previously acknowledged	$2.35
G. W. Drake, Bozeman, Montana,	40

Sada Bailey's Repeal Fund.

Previously acknowledged	1.35
Anna E. Walton, Muscatine, Iowa,	10

Subscribers will please take notice that we now give credit to the "Whole Number" to which payment has been made, so that irregularity of issue will not cause loss of any numbers of the paper.

"La Grippe"-bound and snow-bound, LUCIFER's scribe sends out a feeble greeting this week from the little farm house a mile and a quarter from the office. After a December of phenomenal mildness, and nearly half of January ditto, old Boreas wakened up on the morning of the 12th inst. and for nearly 24 hours blew one of his fiercest blasts, accompanying the same with whirling, drifting, blinding snowflakes. About the same time, or rather preceding by a few days the snow storm, came the Russian Influenza, commonly called "LaGrippe," prostrating and confining to the house a large portion of the citizens of our little city and vicinity. Among the victims of this epidemic disorder, as just stated, is the humble individual who pens these lines.

Masthead of *Lucifer the Light-Bearer* (January 17, 1890).

Masthead of *Lucifer the Light-Bearer* (March 17, 1893).

married woman what she is, a bonded slave, who takes her master's name, her master's bread, her master's commands, and serves her master's passion; who passes through the ordeal of pregnancy and the throes of travail at *his* dictation,—not at her desire; who can control no property, not even her own body, without his consent" (344). A few lines later, she exclaims, "Yes, our Masters! The earth is a prison, the marriage-bed is a cell, women are the prisoners, and you are the keepers!" (344).

De Cleyre's argument that women are stripped of their personhood, both religiously and legally, when they enter into the marriage contract is the basic argument of *Hagar Lyndon*. That women, once they are married, are basically enslaved, both economically and sexually, is the situation that Hagar strives to avoid at all cost. Hagar's mother dies in childbirth with her seventh child, and it is clear that she would not have died if she had not been constantly pregnant and treated as a servant by her "Lord and Master" husband. This is replicated in Hagar's sister's marriage, when she is required to marry a man when she is only fifteen because they were caught together unsupervised. Hagar's sister soon has children, and she and her husband are abusive to each other because of the stress of their earlier marriage and family. The novel suggests that affection, even love, cannot ensure a safe marriage, let alone the room for a woman to have ownership over her own life and body.

Even though Hagar loves her childhood friend Paul, and she wants to become a mother, she cannot bring herself to marry because of the terror her female relatives have experienced as a result of their own marriages. Even the nicest man, Hagar reasons, can turn into a cruel master once the marriage vows have been uttered. It is Hagar's fundamental mistrust of a system of marital bondage that requires complete economic and sexual submission that leads her to become a mother without getting married. And, it is not until she has proven that she can be an individual *and* Paul assures her that they can negotiate their own rules for their marriage that Hagar agrees to marry him.

The intertextual references in the novel also support the idea of women's emancipation from sex slavery. Although the very foundational project of *Hagar Lyndon* is to reject tradition, Holmes draws on symbolism from the Christian *Holy Bible*. In the *Holy Bible*, for instance, Hagar is the Egyptian maid of Sarah. When Sarah is unable to conceive a child, she gives Hagar to her husband, Abraham, so that they may have a child. Hagar gives birth to Ishmael, and the mother and her son are later banished when Ishmael mocks Sarah's child, Issac. Ishmael goes on to found the Ishmaelites, a tribe of what are considered to be Arab peoples. The story of Hagar is the story of a woman rejected from her home who must strike out on her own. By the grace of God, Hagar's son is the progenitor of a new culture, and Holmes uses the same "god-like" and "well-born" descriptions of Hagar's son to describe Hagar Lyndon's son.

Not only is Hagar's name derived from the *Holy Bible*, but so too may be the name of her mother. In Holmes's novel, Hagar's mother is named Martha, a woman who is perpetually pregnant and overworked, and eventually dies from it. In the *Holy Bible*, Jesus visits the house of Martha and her sister Mary. While Martha is busy with her domestic duty of serving, Mary sits at Jesus's feet and listens to him. When Martha complains that Mary is not helping her, Jesus responds that "Mary hath chosen that good part, which shall not be taken away from her," meaning that Mary's actions in listening to Jesus rather than worrying about her domestic duties was the right choice (Luke 10:42). In this scene, Martha is an overworked, domestic figure, and it is Mary who shuns work to listen to Jesus's words. Martha is bogged down in the drudgery of domestic servitude, but it is Mary who chooses to abdicate this role, a choice that is validated by Jesus himself.

Hagar Lyndon also seems to be influenced by writer and reformer Mary Sargeant Gove Nichols's 1855 autobiographical novel *Mary Lyndon, or, Revelations of a Life: An Autobiography*. The victim of a loveless and tyrannical marriage, Mary Lyndon eventually escapes her husband and returns home with her daughter to live with her father. Mary Lyndon's marriage parallels Holmes's Martha Lyndon, where each woman is torn down by working voraciously for the support of the household, a household under which they are servants to their Master husbands. Unlike Holmes's Martha Lyndon, however, Nichols's Mary Lyndon escapes her hellish servitude, and concludes that the only marriage that is fair to women is a marriage in which women have their own physical space in the home and have full control over sexual relations. This is exactly what Martha's daughter Hagar strives for.

According to Joel Myerson in the article "Mary Gove Nichols' *Mary Lyndon*: A Forgotten Reform Novel," Nichols advocated for a similar "free love" philosophy as Holmes does in *Hagar Lyndon*. In a reading of Nichols's novel against popular health reformer Graham, Myerson suggests, "Unlike Graham, Mrs. Nichols argues that a woman has the right to decide with whom she will have sex and how often. While her critics called this promiscuity, she takes it in just the opposite direction. The most important effect of her idea is that a woman can refuse to have sexual relations with her husband" (537). Because women at this time did not have full personhood and were legally considered a man's property, "he could choose to use his property whenever and how many times he wished" (537). Therefore, Nichols's position that women retain autonomy over their own bodies "challenged the marital and legal roles established for women. Her 'free love' effectively meant the freedom *not* to love—or, more specifically, not to *make* love" (Myerson 537). This autonomy is reflected in a kind of oral prenuptial agreement in Mary Lyndon's second marriage.

After her separation from her husband and subsequent love affair with another man, Mary Lyndon tells her soon-to-be second husband, "In a marriage with you, I resign no right of my soul. I enter into no compact to be faithful to you. I only promise to be faithful to the deepest love of my heart…. If my love leads me from you, I must go" (Nichols 385). She further underscores her individual freedom by telling him, "I must have my room, into which none can come, but because I wish it," and he responds, "A woman's right to her room is as imperative as her right to her garments…. I shall only be too happy to come into your room when you desire it" (Nichols 385). Not only does Mary Lyndon insist that marriage and love are two separate entities, she clearly tells her fiancé that she will follow only her heart, and not her marriage vows. Importantly, she further retains her autonomy through her spatial relationship with her husband: having her own room means *she,* not her husband, is in control of if, when, and how sexual acts will take place. The conclusion of Holmes's *Hagar Lyndon* is quite similar to the ending of Nichols's *Mary Lyndon*, albeit without the promise of separate bedrooms. After agreeing to marry Paul, Hagar asks him what will happen if, while married, one of them begins to love someone else: "'But Paul,' Hagar said softly, 'supposing in our feeling of freedom, one of us should sometime love another. Will not the other grieve and die?'" (204). Paul responds with assurances that are hopeful but separate the institution of marriage from love:

> We do not know what may happen—we cannot
> pledge ourselves. Vows would not avert such a fate,
> if it is to come to us. It does not seem possible now.
> I hope we may both enjoy many sweet friendships,
> even loves; yet I believe, I hope that between us
> will be such complete congeniality, such perfect
> understanding, such close sympathy and ready
> response, that no one else ever *can* be to either what
> we are to each other. Between people who are equally
> strong in character, in power to love, in self-reliance,
> who are independent financially and socially, there is
> much more likelihood of a mutual love that is lasting
> than if one is clinging and dependent, the other
> masterful and strong. Ours shall be a new experiment;
> we will *see* if under the best conditions possible in
> the world at present, love *is* lasting and exclusive. Ah,
> Hagar! I have loved you and you only, since you were
> a little child. I am loving you more every day I live. Is
> it likely I shall grow weary of much loving? (204)

Like Mary Lyndon's second marriage, Hagar Lyndon's marriage separates the legal and religious institution of marriage from love and other "sweet friendships." Paul argues that their happiness lies in the fact that they will both be independent and autonomous entities, and, under these "best conditions," he hopes that their love will be "lasting and exclusive," yet fully expects it may not be.

Blaine McKinley reads the ending of *Hagar Lyndon* as a realistic, but also pessimistic, view of the ability of women to transgress the limitations imposed upon them by society. McKinley suggests that even though "for most of its length, *Hagar Lyndon* functions as an anti-domestic novel," "in the end, like the domestic heroine, she learns that she cannot escape from society's restrictions, or her own emotions" ("Free Love" 61). Her inability to escape, McKinley argues, represents Holmes's troubled and pessimistic thinking about the real limitations imposed upon women and the inability to fulfill an anarchist ideology: "Will power is not enough to bring Hagar freedom; a consideration of the limitations of life as a free woman led Holmes to the pessimistic, even fatalistic, conclusion that Hagar must give up her rebellion, accept limits imposed from the outside, and take the best offer she can secure" ("Free Love" 61).

The ending might seem like a defeat to modern readers who may have rooted for Hagar to remain independent and unmarried, but this ending gives Hagar the best of both worlds: She is able to gain some semblance of respectability within the larger community, retain her autonomy, and co-habitate with the man she truly does love, without the danger of being tied to him forever in servitude, and with the acknowledgement that they may grow to love other people. While radical by even today's standards of normalcy, this would have given a solution to women who saw the inevitable tension between marriage and retaining their intellectual and bodily autonomy. In fact, in her 2003 book *Sex Radicals and the Quest for Women's Equality*, Joanne E. Passett takes a less negative position than McKinley. She argues that "In *Hagar Lyndon*, Holmes explores the question of whether or not a woman can live freely in an unfree environment. Her narrative critiques existing social customs and economic realities governing women's lives and illustrates her vision of an ideal world and the impediments that stood in the way of its lasting achievement" (154). Instead of reading the ending as a failure as McKinley does, Passett maintains that the text ends with uncertainty: "The story ends on an ambiguous note, with Hagar attempting to negotiate a relationship with [Paul] Deane that would preserve both her identity and her ability to act freely" (155). Moreover, Passett argues, "In Hagar Lyndon, female readers [of *Lucifer*] found a woman they could admire, someone who possessed the means, the courage to practice the principles they endorsed" (155).

Positioned in between McKinley and Passett, Holly Jackson, in her article "The Marriage Trap in the Free-Love Novel and Queer Critique," identifies the ending of *Hagar Lyndon* as neither radical nor liberatory; rather, Jackson argues, marriage becomes a refuge for Hagar, providing "legal and social protections" without which Hagar's extramarital life would be limited (697). And, as Jackson contends, we never do find out if Hagar and Paul negotiate and act out a marriage arrangement that would, as Passett puts it, allow Hagar to "live freely in an unfree environment."

Although Lizzie Holmes did not write regional fiction, or fiction that illustrates and comments on the way people behave in regionally specific ways, *Hagar Lyndon* is a story of the Midwest, both in its setting and its readership. Originally from Ohio, Holmes moved to Chicago in the 1880s and was well-aware of not only the small-town atmosphere that Hagar grows up in but also the liberating capacities of growing urban centers like Chicago. The very first line of the novel places the reader in a little town in the Midwest:

> A little, common place village stood on the banks of
> a pretty stream in one of the middle states; a village
> which contained the usual "post-office, store and
> blacksmith shop," two or three rival churches, one
> principal street and several small cross streets; whose
> inhabitants were of the ordinary village type—people
> strongly addicted to old customs and habits, with
> set opinions, deep prejudices and tendencies toward
> intense condemnation of all things wicked (1).

Many of *Lucifer*'s readers lived in small towns just like the one Holmes sets up here, and often the periodical was their only lifeline to radical ideas. Holmes wrote what she knew, but the setting of *Hagar Lyndon* in a small town in the Midwest was important to illustrate to her readers that she recognizes the horrors of sex slavery do exist. Even in these common but idyllic Midwestern villages where religion is supposed to be the only moral compass, its citizens can grow up to become radical women, like Hagar. Hagar's moral and intellectual growth as well as her escape from this village would be a cue to readers that they are not alone.

Upon its publication, the feedback from *Lucifer* readers was overwhelmingly positive for *Hagar Lyndon*, with readers writing in to the "Various Voices" section and sending in their own full-length reviews and letters. Lois Waisbrooker's review, published in the July

28, 1893 issue—the issue that also published Chapters 17 and 18 of *Hagar Lyndon*—gives key insight to its critical reception. She weighs in on the important didactic, or teaching, purpose of the novel:

> More than thirty years ago, a school teacher lived what the writer of Hagar Lyndon represents her heroine doing. There women that I have known have deliberately chosen motherhood, and after a time accepted wifehood, but in the story now being published in LUCIFER's columns, I find for the first time woman's inalienable right to motherhood without entering into bonds, and I am glad to see it—glad to read it. It is not exactly what independent motherhood will be when woman is recognized for what she is. In the now perverted state of things, she may think it best to fight her battle without the aid of her child's father, but when the battle is fought and won, she can then have his presence and loving support without being in any sense owned, and she will realize that in justice to her child she should have that support. But I am glad Hagar Lyndon is being born into the world of literature. The seed being sown will bear fruit in the future, and then we shall have intelligent and honored motherhood. (2)

Waisbrooker was both a forerunner and contemporary to Lizzie Swank Holmes, and was opinionated and prolific on the subject of emancipated motherhood. In fact, before her brief stint as editor of *Lucifer* in the early 1890s, she appeared frequently in its pages as an author and in letters to the editor. Like Holmes, Waisbrooker wrote sentimental fiction with themes about the emancipation of women, the slavery of women and men in loveless marriages, and the right of women to be good and proud mothers without marrying. Many of Waisbrooker's novels, which were widely advertised and referenced in the pages of *Lucifer*, pre-date *Hagar Lyndon* by as much as twenty-four years and could have paved the way for Holmes's conception of her work. Three of her more well-known novels, *Alice Vale: A Story for the Times*, *Helen Harlow's Vow*,

EMANCIPATION

OF

WOMANHOOD AND MOTHERHOOD

From their Present Condition of Enslavement to Man-made Laws and Customs, Including Civil Disabilities, Industrial and Economic Discriminations, and, above all, Sexual Subordination and Subjugation to the Caprice of Man as Her Divinely-ordained Lord and Master.

Among the books offered by LUCIFER treating upon this class of subjects we give prominence to the following:

PERFECT MOTHERHOOD, or Mabel Raymond's Resolve. By Lois Waisbrooker. Price, $1.00.

HELEN HARLOW'S VOW. By Lois Waisbrooker. Price, $1.00.

IRENE, or The Road to Freedom. By Sada B. Fowler. Price, $1. The same with LUCIFER one year, $1.90.

THE WOMAN WHO DARES. By Ursula Gestefeld. $1.25. The same with LUCIFER one year, $2.

A CITYLESS AND COUNTRYLESS WORLD. By Henry Olerich. $1. With LUCIFER one year, $1.90.

OCCULT FORCES OF SEX. Waisbrooker. 50 cents.

A SEX REVOLUTION. Same author. 25 cents.

THE STRIKE OF A SEX. By G. N. Miller. 25 cents.

RADICAL REMEDY in Social Science. Dr. E. B. Foote jr. 25c.

LAW OF POPULATION. By Anna Besant. 15 and 25 cents.

CUPID'S YOKES. By Ezra H. Heywood. 15 cents.

DIANA. 25 cents.

DISCUSSION of the SOCIAL QUESTION. Severance-Jones. 15c.

THE PRODIGAL DAUGHTER. By Rachel Campbell. 10c.

DAUGHTERS OF CAIN. Mrs. M. A. Freeman. 50c.

Marriage and Divorce. A. E. Giles. 10c.

Horrors of Modern Matrimony. By Dr. Robert Greer. 15c.

Autonomistic Marriage. Kelso. 5c.

Reform of a Century. 20c.

Betrayed. Voltairine de Cleyre. 5c.

His Confession. Same author. 5c.

A Good Man Sent to Prison. Pentecost. 5c.

The Philosophy of Disease, and How to Cure the Sick Without Drugs. By Juliet Severance, M. D. 15c.

Next Revolution. Nos. 1, 2, 3 and 4. 10c each.

What Diana Teaches. 2c.

Titles offered by *Lucifer the Light-Bearer* on the subject of "Emancipation, Or, Womanhood and Motherhood" (*Lucifer the Light-Bearer*, June 16, 1893).

and *Perfect Motherhood; or Mabel Raymond's Resolve* revolve around plots of women who have had a child outside of marriage and demand justice from public scorn. In her review of *Hagar Lyndon*, Waisbrooker acknowledges that Hagar Lyndon chooses to have a child outside of the bonds of marriage. She recognizes that doing so would not be easy, and writes, "it is not exactly what independent motherhood will be when woman is recognized for what she is," but it is certainly a step in the right direction and a good lesson for the women reading to show that it can be done.

On the same page of *Lucifer* directly adjacent to Waisbrooker's glowing review is a letter from M.S.L. She or he first responds to criticism from some readers that *Hagar Lyndon* is "overdrawn," or what we would call today too "overdone" or "unbelievable." M.S.L, however, disagrees with this criticism, and backs the argument up with a story about her or his own mother:

As direct statement is better than mere inference, I
will give proof of a parallel case of 'Mrs. Lyndon.' My
mother, daughter of a rich man, cultured, refined and
educated, though being governed by that superstition
called, the Christian religion, gave herself up through
marriage to my father, another *Mr.* 'John Lyndon.'
And nearer to him in his daily manifestation than in
name even. He exercised all the prerogatives that the
church and a strongly sexed Hebrew god gave him.
In a few short years she bore, by my father, and grace
of god, eight children—my sister, a few years younger
and I alone surviving. "God called the rest home,"
said my father and the pious neighbors. Died for lack
of vitality, was the physician's verdict.

My poor mother dragged out life 'a patient,
obedient exemplary wife.' Till last winter, then my
father lost a slave. 'Died of a husband' would be a
suitable inscription for her headstone. She was strong,
reliant and fairly logical till any one questioned the
sanctity of the marriage relation. Then reason fled
before former superstition. Nor is her case isolated.
I have met so many, and many I meet daily who live

the curse of Christian marriage through to the truly
bitter end. (2–3)

These two letters illustrate just how descriptive *Hagar Lyndon*
was of the problems that faced women in the late nineteenth
century. Because the nineteenth century was a time before the
standard birth control methods in use today, for women of child-
bearing age, sexual relations almost always meant pregnancy and
motherhood. Both Waisbrooker and M.S.L identify *Hagar Lyndon*'s
separation of enforced sexual relations through marriage and
motherhood. In a time before sure-fire birth control, motherhood
outside of marriage was birth control, allowing women to be
mothers when they wanted to, not because they were forced
into sexual relations by husbands invoking their "marital rights."
It is important to remember, too, that women like Holmes,
Waisbrooker, and especially Voltarine de Cleyre are calling
"enforced motherhood" and "enforced marital relations" rape. At
this time in history, if a woman was raped by her husband, and
often by any man who had any kind of authority over her, either
legally or socially, she had no recourse. The coded language of these
letters, especially the use of the words "enforced motherhood," is an
attempt to explain to women that rape should not be a normal part
of any sexual relationship, in marriage or otherwise.

Eugenics and Free Love

Although today's readers may be sympathetic to Hagar's desire for
independence, they may be less enthusiastic about the eugenicist
themes of the novel. Many of Holmes's contemporaries, such as
Lois Waisbrooker, argue for "free love" or motherhood outside
of marriage because it would create a healthier, more fit child.
Although *Hagar Lyndon* is not an explicitly eugenicist text, Hagar's
child is portrayed as exceptionally fit because of its parentage,
not in spite of it. In fact, in a conversation with some snooty
women in the town who are scandalized at the thought of Hagar's
"illegitimate" child, Hagar's doctor proclaims that Hagar's baby is
"A little beauty—strong, healthy, perfect" (154). To their shock,
he follows up his evaluation with an endorsement of Hagar's life

choices: "Let any one of you show me a child welcomed, born of loving, healthy parents, whose mother knows how to take care of herself, and I'll show you another such a beauty. Such a child is truly 'well born,' an aristocrat among babies" (154). Not only is Hagar's baby fit in eugenics terms, it occupies a privileged position similar to that bestowed by class by virtue of its fitness.

Holmes also compares Hagar's baby to a "small god" that Hagar worships: "The small god was a constant wonder. She kissed its pink soft skin, on cheek, brow, lips and hands, and gazed in awed rapture and surprise; that tiny, lovely creature was part of herself. Surely every birth is a miraculous conception" (155–56). Hagar is enamoured with her baby, but also understands there is something special about him. Not only is her baby "well born," but he is an object of worship: he becomes a Christ-like figure. Moreover, Hagar becomes Mary, further distancing sex from reproduction, an important distinction for many free lovers for whom the focus was not on the sexual act but that ability to have control over the who, when, and where of motherhood.

For many, including many of the readers of *Lucifer*, having fit children was a more important reason for women to be able to have children outside of marriage than for the health and welfare of the mother herself. In other words, one of the primary driving factors of "free love," or the ability for women to have sex, and thus children, outside of marriage, was to improve the fitness of the race. This theme helps us to understand why Moses Harman decided to turn *Lucifer* into *The American Journal of Eugenics* thirteen years after the publication of *Hagar Lyndon*.

In 1907, the same year the United States' first eugenics law was enacted in Indiana, *Lucifer the Light-Bearer* became *The American Journal of Eugenics*. Eugenics, or the broad philosophy of selective reproduction (including sterilization) to engineer a "fitter" human race, is an underlying theme that runs throughout the pages of *Lucifer* even in its nineteenth-century form. Even still in 1910, Harman was advertising *Lucifer* as the forbearer of *The American Journal of Eugenics*. The journal proclaims, "The American Journal of Eugenics formerly known as Lucifer the Light Bearer" is "the Pioneer Journal—in Modern Times—of an old and almost forgotten science, the most important of all sciences, a science successfully and openly taught and practiced by the ancient Greeks and Egyptians, but ignored, defeated, scorned, out-lawed by all modern nations, viz., the Science of Right-Borning, the Science of GOOD GENERATION" (48). This advertisement connects the previous pro-woman focus of *Lucifer* with the journal's new eugenics focus: "Its central thought is Natural Selection through Freedom of Motherhood, the Self-ownership of Woman in the Realm of Sex and Reproduction—Intelligent and Responsible Parenthood; Woman First, Man Second" (48).

In the twentieth century, *eugenics* emerged as a term closely associated with the sterilization of unfit or criminal individuals, usually without their consent or against their will. The "unfit" individuals most likely to be sterilized were poor, non-white, uneducated, incarcerated, and differently-abled. After New Deal reforms that provided a better safety net for the poor and working-class, doctors and politicians often suggested that sterilization was a way to keep those from lower-socioeconomic strata of society from becoming a drain on the government, whether that be through programs like welfare, special education, or incarceration. *Hagar Lyndon* illustrates the genesis of a seemingly innocuous social practice that would go on to violate the rights and change the lives of millions of Americans.

Although commonly believed to have died out with the knowledge of the atrocities committed by Nazi Germany leading up to and during WWII, forcible sterilization actually increased in the United States after this time. According to Gregory Michael Dorr,

> The federal government, responsible for subsidizing this cottage industry in sterilization, admitted that 16,000 women and 9,000 men had been sterilized at public expense between 1972 and 1973. Government officials, however, could not vouch for the degree of informed consent in every case. Black women had special reason for concern. Beyond the conventional wisdom about 'Mississippi appendectomies' in the black community (sterilizations performed under the guise of other abdominal surgeries), independent studies demonstrated in 1970 that black women were sterilized at more than twice the rate of white women. (174)

Further Work

Unlike some of the other fiction and non-fiction published in the pages of *Lucifer the Light-Bearer*, Holmes's *Hagar Lyndon* was not republished as a complete work after its serialization. This is unusual in that re-printing pamphlets, short essays, poetry, and fiction that appeared in the pages of *Lucifer* was part of the overall economic plan of the periodical. In many of the early issues, there is a special advertisement section that lists many of the reprinted stand-alone works that first appeared in the newspaper, as well as other titles of interest for sale through the periodical's office. It is unclear why *Hagar Lyndon* was never reprinted as a stand-alone edition, especially given its hearty endorsement by the likes of Waisbrooker and the intense discussion it generated in the periodical itself. Whatever the case, *Hagar Lyndon* lived on only through a set of microfilmed images housed at the Kansas State Historical Society, further linking the novel's past and future with the historical legacy of the Midwest.

Scholarship on Lizzie Swank Holmes is relatively non-existent at the moment, mostly owing to the fact that her only known novel, *Hagar Lyndon,* was virtually inaccessible for over one-hundred years. However, she enjoyed a long and productive career in publishing. Recently, burgeoning interest in anarchist-feminist recovery work and archival digitization has revealed over one-hundred essays and stories published between 1884 and 1912 in a range of periodicals under both her own name and her pen name "May Huntley." Anarchist historian Shawn P. Wilbur is one of the driving forces in the recovery work. Once considered a minor figure in Chicago and anarchist history, Lizzie Swank Holmes is beginning to emerge as an important historical and literary figure in her own right.

Works Cited

De Cleyre, Voltairine. "They Who Marry Do Ill." *The Selected Works of Voltairine de Cleyre: Poems, Essays, Sketches and Stories, 1885–1911*. Ed. Alexander Berkman. Oakland: AK Press, 2016.

Dorr, Gregory Michael. "Protection or Control? Women's Health, Sterilization Abuse, and *Relf v. Weinberger*." *A Century of Eugenics in America: From the Indiana Experiment to the Human Genome Era*. Ed. Paul A. Lombardo. Bloomington: Indiana UP, 2011. 161–190.

Green, James. *Death in the Haymarket: A Story of Chicago, the First Labor Movement and the Bombing that Divided Gilded Age America*. Anchor Books, 2006.

Holmes, Lizzie Swank. *Hagar Lyndon* [1893]. Hastings, Nebraska: Hastings College Press, 2018.

———. "'Let No Man Falter' Says Lizzie Holmes." *The Labor World* 16 Mar. 1907: 1.

———. "Revolutionists" from *Free Society* 2 Nov. 1899. In *Haymarket Scrapbook*. Eds. Dave Roediger and Franklin Rosemont. Chicago: Charles H. Kerr, 1986/AK Press, 2012. 179–180.

The Holy Bible. Authorized King James Version. Oxford UP, 2008.

Jackson, Holly. "The Marriage Trap in the Free-Love Novel and Queer Critique." *American Literature* 87.4 (2015): 681–708.

McKinley, Blaine. "Free Love and Domesticity: Lizzie M. Holmes, *Hagar Lyndon* (1893), and the Anarchist-Feminist Imagination." *Journal of American Culture* 13.1 (1990): 55–62.

———. "Holmes, Lizzie May Swank." *Women Building Chicago 1790–1990: A Biographical Dictionary*. Eds. Rima Lunin Schultz and Adele Hast. Bloomington: Indiana UP, 2001: 400–402.

M.S.L. Untitled Letter in "Various Voices." *Lucifer the Light-Bearer*. 28 July 1893: 3–4.

Marsh, Margaret S. *Anarchist Women, 1870–1920*. Temple UP, 1981.

Myerson, Joel. "Mary Gove Nichols' *Mary Lyndon*: A Forgotten Reform Novel." *American Literature* 58.4 (1986): 523–539.

Nichols, Mary Sargeant Gove. *Mary Lyndon; or, Revelations of a Life: An Autobiography*. New York: Stringer and Townsend, 1855. Accessed through *Archive.org*.

Passett, Joanne E. *Sex Radicals and the Quest for Women's Equality*. U of Illinois P, 2003.

Sears, Hal D. *The Sex Radicals: Free Love in High Victorian America.* Regents Press of Kansas, 1977.

Waisbrooker, Lois. "Hagar Lyndon." *Lucifer the Light-Bearer.* 28 July 1893: 3.

Michelle M. Campbell is a doctoral candidate in nineteenth-century American literature at Purdue University in West Lafayette, Indiana. Her current research focuses on nineteenth-century Midwestern anarchist women writers. She is a member of the Society for the Study of Midwestern Literature and the North American Anarchist Studies Network. Her work has appeared in *Anarchist Developments in Cultural Studies* and *MidAmerica.*

"Long ages gone she laid
Under the ban
In Eden's garden made
Subject to man.
Now as the dawning light greets her sad eyes
Comes the awakening thought 'Might I not rise?'"

I

The Sanctity of the Home

A little, common place village stood on the banks of a pretty stream in one of the middle states; a village which contained the usual "post-office, store and blacksmith shop," two or three rival churches, one principal street and several small cross streets; whose inhabitants were of the ordinary village type—people strongly addicted to old customs and habits, with set opinions, deep prejudices and tendencies toward intense condemnation of all things wicked.

Toward one end of the principal street stood a plain brown cottage, the home of James Lyndon. The house contained his wife and six children also, but these were of no particular importance in the community. Mr. Lyndon himself, though but an overseer in a flouring mill, was a greatly respected citizen, a deacon in his church, one of the town trustees, a model before all the younger men, of stern and strict integrity. No one exactly loved him, but that did not matter, respect and deference are better than affection to some men. He was always at his post, wherever that might be: on Sunday three times at church; during working hours, frowning and giving orders somewhere in the mill; in the evenings, he could ever be found in the "bosom of his family." Mr. Lyndon possessed all the virtues—and yet contributed as little happiness to the human race in general as a man well could and live. No word of complaint ever passed the lips of wife or children; but her sad, white face, and their cowed wistful looks told a silent story of their own.

One evening, in the fall of the year, the father and four children were seated at the supper table. Mrs. Lyndon was still attending to something on the stove, carrying a baby on one hip while she hastily worked with the free hand.

"Martha!" called out the husband and father in a stern voice. "You know I will not have this fussing about when you have once said the meal is ready. Sit down."

"Yes directly—I only wanted a moment"—and she sat down nervously with inward misgiving as to spoons and salt and the insufficient steeping of the tea.

"Where is Lucy?"

Mrs. Lyndon looked up depreciatingly. "I had to send her to the store for a few little things for breakfast. I think I heard her come in the back way a minute ago—she is probably cleaning her rubbers and will be in in a moment."

Mr. Lyndon scowled. "A very shiftless, loose way of doing things. You should think of everything you will need when you order your groceries, and never send a child out for a "few little things" so near night. Never let it happen again. We will wait just two minutes for her."

Two minutes of absolute, dreary silence ensued. The potatoes steamed away their heat and the meat plate cooled while the hungry children looking longingly at the vanishing vapors. Then the father angrily bowed his head and pronounced a vindictive sounding "grace." The meal proceeded in silence. Mrs. Lyndon's face grew paler and more anxious every moment; the quiet children ate what was given them without a word, and the head of the house seemed to dispense gloom and foreboding with every mouthful.

Nearest Mrs. Lyndon sat a girl of twelve. She often glanced up at her mother's face with a serious, comprehensive sympathy beyond her years. She was a slight and slender child, with a thin, sallow face—a wonderful face however, lighted by great fathomless dark eyes that thrilled one with their mysteries and possibilities—a sad, serious old-looking face that haunted one.

"Hagar," the mother whispered to her when the meal came to an end. "Keep Johnnie still a little while—I want to go out a few minutes."

The little girl quickly assumed charge of the child and the mother went to a side table pretending to be doing some work there. When Mr. Lyndon's back was turned she grabbed a shawl and noiselessly slipped out of the back door. But he soon missed her.

"Hagar where has your mother gone?"

"I don't know sir," answered the little girl gently, patting the baby who was beginning to whimper.

"There is some kind of deviltry going on. That girl not in yet and the mother deceiving me and dodging about. I'll have to give this family a lesson or two yet."

With a heavy stride and threatening looks he put on his coat and hat and started out of the front door. Outside a moonless night was settling down; a cool wind rattled the crisp, fading leaves of trees and shrubbery and the few street lamps seemed to burn dimly in a discouraged sort of way. A lane crossed the street on which the Lyndon's lived not far from their gate. At the corner, a great beech tree with low hanging branches grew and cast a shadow beneath that was always heavy. Toward this Mr.

Lyndon hurried. A moment before a woman's form well wrapt up had glided swiftly up from the other direction; he did not see it, but as he was about to go on, he heard a low voice in the shadow.

"Lucy, go quickly—run to the back door—your father—" the rest was lost. Then came an unintelligible word in a man's voice.

"The devil!" this pious man ejaculated as he made a dash into the darkness. He caught a young man by the collar and gave him a fling without looking to see where he landed; grasped a young girl by the shoulders, gave her a terrific shaking then pushed her in front of him until they reached his own door when, opening it, he flung her inside. The slight woman with her head wrapt in a shawl followed, trembling and silent.

"I'll teach you to disobey me you young hussy! I told you never to speak to that wicked scamp again. You are forbidden to be out of the house after dark, and here I find you hiding behind a tree in the night with the worst rascal in town. I'll cure you, Miss."

He reached for a long slender black whip which hung on the wall.

Lucy, a well grown girl scarcely fifteen had picked herself up and stood facing him. Her sullen defiant face with its flashing black eyes and flaming cheeks possessed the sort of beauty that aggravated her father. He liked to see women quiet, meek and colorless—that brilliant, dashing look, too early matured, he considered in itself a crying sin and ought to be whipt out of the girl. He gave her a fierce blow across the shoulders.

"James!" cried the mother piteously. "Don't! I'm sure she will never disobey you again. Oh don't whip her—that will never cure her—leave her to me, I'll talk to her."

"*You*, madam! You are scarcely fit to speak to your children much less teach them. A woman who will lie to her husband to screen his children in their wrong doing, who will encourage them in disgracing themselves, needs disciplining herself. Badness runs in your family. Your daughters, if they depended on your guidance alone, would follow in the footsteps of your wicked, fallen sister, and God knows what you would have been if I hadn't married you and kept you straight."

A momentary fire crept into the weary eyes. "James, do you insult me before our children? You know our family is a most honorable one, and never knew disgrace until poor Clive so unfortunately trusted—"

"Silence woman! How dare you answer me back? I'll attend to your case presently."

He turned toward his daughter again and raised the whip.

"James! You must not! Think of it. Our first born, almost a woman, to strike her like a brute—" she laid a beseeching hand on his harm. He struck it off and gave her a violent push. The poor woman's short lived daring deserted her; she caught herself from falling, took up her baby and bent her tearful face low over its soft and tender one. There was nothing more she could do— the mother heart must bleed in vain, while a heavy hand rained blows upon her first born. What she had so dreaded was passing now and she could do nothing. Ah! you who write so beautifully of romantic sorrows and picture human woe in scenes of tender pathos or deep tragedy, take for your next subject, a soft hearted mother sitting helplessly by while the child for whom she has suffered is undergoing a "good thrashing." It is not a romantic, a novel or a beautiful theme, but the pathetic and helpless agony is deep enough for the most eloquent pen.

The crying girl is finally sent off up stairs to bed without a light and without her supper. The other frightened children steal away—except Hagar who creeps nearer her mother and furtively smooths her hair. The little caress is answered with a like one.

"Put down that child. A woman who will do what you have tonight needs time and opportunity to reflect on her conduct. Get up and walk into that room."

Mechanically, as though long accustomed to obedience, and not thinking what it meant Martha Lyndon walked through the door her husband held open for her. It led into a small, cheerless store-room containing only boxes, bags, cans and barrels of provisions. The door slammed shut, Lyndon turned the key and put it in his pocket. Hagar's dark solemn eyes grew big and bright and threatening as she stood opposite him with the large baby in her delicate arms, until he could not look at her steadily; there was something awesome and ominous in the little, thin, womanish face, with her great strange eyes through which an unknown soul seemed to gaze. He could not bear her near him. It was a little strange that though she possessed less of his love than any of his children he had never struck or punished her other than to send her from the room.

"Take the baby to bed with you and go," he said gruffly and Hagar silently obeyed. Then he took down the family bible, opened it out upon the table, where he had pushed aside some of the dishes, and sat down before it. Whatever happened the evening's reading and prayers were never neglected; though the whole family was in disgrace and unfit to be present, he would conduct the exercises alone. He retired at the usual time without speaking, or hearing a sound from the locked store-room.

The house was perfectly still as the night hours crept on. If he had only known it, his wife in her chilly, uncomfortable prison seated on a bag of bran was not unhappy at being there. She knew of more disagreeable ways of spending a night, and just now she was very glad of a locked door between her lord and master and herself.

Toward morning the baby began to cry. Hagar had never closed her eyes, but had been sitting up in her little bed watching her brother and thinking, thinking. Now she tried to hush him but found she could not, she arose and with the baby in her arms, raked up the dying embers in the kitchen stove, put on some milk to warm, then tried to feed him. But he would not be satisfied in that way. For the first time in his short life he missed the loving mother's breast and soothing voice and found that crying would not bring them.

"Hagar," softly called the mother, "can't you contrive some way to unlock the door and give me baby?"

"How can I mother? There is no key."

"A crooked nail might do, or try one of the other door keys."

"I don't think I can open it with any of these. Shall I wake father?"

"No, no. Try any other way."

"Wait a moment; I know."

Hagar placed the baby in his cradle and ran noiselessly to her father's room. The door was ajar and stealing in on tip-toe she found his clothes and carefully hunted for the key. It was a courageous, a terrible thing—it was disobedience, theft, disgrace, but Hagar never hesitated. If she had known he would wake and kill her she would have done it just the same. But he slept heavily and never knew she was there. A few moments more and the store-room door was open.

"Now mother come to my bed. We can manage to squeeze in together and baby can lie on your arm."

"No Hagar I'll go back where he locked me and save trouble for both of us."

When her baby was once more quietly sleeping, Mrs. Lyndon laid him down in Hagar's bed. Then she softly stole up stairs to gaze with a mother's pitying eyes on the flushed, tear-stained face of Lucy in her uneasy slumbers. Poor mother! Poor Lucy! She could only gently kiss her and pour a flood of sweet sympathy about her unconscious form.

"Now Hagar dear, give me a pillow and a blanket, lock my prison door, put the key back carefully, then go to sleep, there's a good child."

"Oh mother must you go back?"

"Hush! Kiss me goodnight."

Hagar did as she was bid and successfully replaced the key. And then the wearied girl slept.

II

A Disgrace to the Family

No signs of civil war were visible in the household the next day; the family, being "a well-regulated" one, scenes were smoothed over and forgotten as soon as possible. There might have been a rebellious light in Lucy's handsome eyes, but she seemed subdued and docile enough. She had something of the stubborn and aggressive disposition of her father; like a fighter when beaten, she took her whipping quietly but immediately went into training for a new encounter. She possessed none of that sensitiveness or spirituality that belonged to her mother and sister, which made a blow a calamity scarcely to be recovered from in a lifetime. It was

not the first time it had occurred, and she only hated her father a
little more intensely after each punishment.

Hagar was a silent child. No one but her mother knew
how keen was her comprehension of every day's occurrences, how
deep was her unspoken sympathy and how serious her thoughts
of life. A realizing sense of humanity's sorrows had settled upon
her perceptive mind too early; it is a sad thing for a child to
become wise so young. The "bliss of ignorance," the repose of
perfect trust can never be theirs in all their lives; for later in life
ignorance is *not* bliss and confidence can*not* be implicit. Hagar
played as other children do, only enough to amuse the younger
ones; she read every thing readable within her reach, and sat
silently and meditated whenever she could; but work and school
occupied much of her time. She had one good friend among
her schoolmates, who did not resent her unsociable ways, but
succeeded often in drawing her out to speak of her thoughts in a
quiet way. His father kept a few books in a small store of notions,
and many of these were surreptitiously transferred to Hagar's
hands and back again without any one being the wiser. She felt
no scruples in obtaining her reading in this way, or in hiding
from her father the fact that she thus read many forbidden works.
In a vague way she felt that no one had any right to interfere
with her mental pursuits; she calmly brushed away every obstacle
that stood between her and the intellectual food she craved by

any means in her power without conscientious pang. She was
of the stuff of which martyrs are made. She would have died
before she would do anything *she* considered cruel, cowardly or
dishonorable; but her ideas of ethics were original and peculiar—
entirely her own.

She was walking from school one day talking to her friend,
Paul Deane, when an unusually showy carriage drawn by a
matched pair of horses drew up to the walk. An elegantly dressed
lady leaned out and spoke her name.

"Why, who is it?" murmured Hagar half to herself.
Something familiar in the face attracted her, and she looked until
a memory of that same face, wan and white, with the dark grey
eyes full of despair, came back to her. The woman had then worn
a faded calico dress and a thin shawl, now her dress was of silk
and plush; she looked prosperous and handsome—a little hard
and defiant perhaps, but a latent gleam of human kindness lurked
in her changeable grey eyes.

"You are my Aunt Clive Daley, aren't you?"

"Yes, dear, that's who I am. I didn't think you would
remember me. I am awfully glad to see you, and would like to
take you right in here with me and give you a good hug and kiss,
then a nice long ride afterward—but I suppose it wouldn't do.
How are mother and Lucy and Ben—and how many more babies
are there?"

"Three since you saw us. We are all well, only—well, mother never complains, but she doesn't look strong. I am glad to see you Aunt Clive. Why can't I ride with you?"

Miss Daley laughed—a hard and mocking laugh and said, "What would good Deacon Lyndon say? I rather guess not, little one. You know I am forbidden the house, but I wish I could see your mother only for a few minutes. Couldn't she steal out and meet me somewhere?"

"Poor mother, she has so much trouble any way—it would worry her so much to risk it I don't like to tell her. But I'm quite sure she would send her love and good wishes."

"Oh well, I scarcely dared to hope it, though I came here for no other reason. I live in M———, (a city about fifty miles from the village), and could not resist running down to see the 'home of my childhood,' though it has no sweet recollections for me. Here's something to buy poor Mattie some comforts—I'll warrant you she needs lots of things she can't get, and goodby dear Hagar," and she threw a little purse into Hagar's hands as she gathered up the reins to drive away. Hagar looked at the pretty plush and gold affair with pleasure. Some comforts for mother from her sister's abundance seemed perfectly correct to her.

"I wouldn't take that, if I were you," said Paul gravely.

"Why not? Aunt Clive seems to be rich, and well able to afford it."

Paul Deane was fifteen, and had learned more of the world's moral code than had Hagar.

"It is the price of shame. It is not honestly earned."

"I don't believe it, Paul Deane. My aunt does not look one bit ashamed, and I know she is kind-hearted and good, and wouldn't steal a cent from anybody. If any one gives her money they give it willingly,"

"Yes, of course, but you will learn why some day."

"I don't see anything wrong in it, and ma will be glad to find Aunt Clive remembers her now she is well off. I'm going home." And swift as a bird Hagar ran down the road until she reached the house. Habitual care about "waking the baby," made her pause a moment before entering, and when she did, to look and see what mother was doing before she interrupted her. The tired looking mother was rocking the cradle with one foot while she patched children's clothes heaped upon her lap; the next two younger children were playing with blocks by her side.

"Mother, who do you think I've just seen? She sent her love, and gave me this to buy a present for you, and looked handsome and well, and wore such a beautiful dress, and rode in a splendid carriage—aren't you glad she has grown so rich?"

"Who—who, Hagar? Not Clive, surely?"

"Yes, it was Aunt Clive, and she wishes she could see you——"

"Poor sister! Poor dear Clive!" murmured Mrs. Lyndon, leaning back in her chair trembling and faint.

"What is it mother? Are you sick?"

"No, but I am startled to hear of my unfortunate sister again. Oh, dear! The poor girl must have gone wrong entirely. I wish I might see her, but that is impossible I suppose. And we used to love each other so much."

"How has she 'gone wrong entirely'? She looked to me as though she had gone the other way. What is it, mother, that Aunt Clive has done that every one thinks she is so bad?"

"I don't know that you could understand all of the sad story, but I will try to tell you. Long ago, when she was a merry girl of eighteen, Clive loved a man very much and they were engaged to be married; she believed in him and trusted him, and because they were too young and too poor to marry right away, he persuaded her to be as though they were. Then he went away after awhile without telling any one, and none of us has ever heard of him since. Then—after awhile a sweet little baby was born to Clive. But she had no home—we were orphans and poor working girls—and she was sick in a charity hospital. I wanted to bring her here, but your father would not hear of such a thing. She had to wander about the country carrying her baby and begging for a few mouthfuls to eat, and a shelter in some barn at night. Finally the baby died, and from nothing but hunger and exposure. Clive came here then and begged your father to let her stay a few days and rest. He refused her, called her bad names, and said she must never come near his house again. I cried and pleaded for her as I never have pleaded for anything for myself, but it only seemed to anger him the more. She said some terrible things to him, that he was responsible for her baby's death, and more—I can't tell you all. But she went away—so poorly dressed—so despairing, so weak and sick, it has haunted me ever since. I am glad to know she is comfortable, but I tremble to think of the price she must have paid."

Hagar's eyes were full of tragic wonder as she listened.

"I can't see anything bad in what she did. Only the people were so cruel as to let a little baby die of hunger and cold were bad. Oh, how could anybody do that? To let a poor, sweet baby suffer for care until it died! I cannot bear to think of it."

Tears were streaming down Hagar's cheeks. Her mother regretted having told her the tale, for her little daughter fairly *lived* every story of suffering she ever heard.

"Don't think of it, dear. It is all over and past now, and Clive is comfortable."

"Oh! Clive—she might have been happy if she had had a home. Just think! A dear baby to love, all her own, and no father to come and worry and make them both afraid. And just one baby! Not too many, so that she would get tired out and not love any of them enough. I should think that would be so nice."

"Why, Hagar, how strangely you talk!"

"Well, isn't it true? I know you get so tired of us all, you look so pale sometimes. Do you know I often stop and think of you in school—always I know you are here in the shabby rooms, all the time doing something for Johnnie, or Bennie, or Mary, or fixing something right so father won't scold when he comes home. You never go anywhere except to that tiresome church, that you have to hurry yourself to death to get ready for. You never have any fun, you never talk much to anybody, and—you've always got father's coming home to expect at night."

The look on Hagar's expressive face showed there was no bright anticipation in that thought to her.

"*Don't* you get awfully tired of such a lot of us? If you could get away sometimes—if you could have something to go to that is what our school is to us, for I don't suppose you have learned everything, mother? and forget the work and worry we make you——"

"Oh, hush child! It is wicked to think such things. A woman's place is in her own home caring for her children—what else is there in life? There, do not think of it any more—mother never gets tired of you, anyway."

Hagar moved away in a thoughtful mood as Lucy ran noisily in, her hair in jaunty confusion under a smart little hat, and her cheeks and eyes all aglow.

"Lucy," said her mother anxiously, "I am afraid you have been talking to Dan Mason again."

"Well, yes I have. He met me on the street and walked with me a little ways. I don't care. Father won't let me go anywhere, not even to a little party or a meeting after night. I can't have any company, or have any fun, or see anybody I'd like to see. I can't endure such a life. I'll go wild if I can't break the monotony a little bit once in a while. I don't care particularly for Dan Mason. I like the young fellows who belong to the club and go to dances, and hold debating schools, much better. But I never can go where they are and they never see me excepting by chance in my old clothes when I dursn't say a word. What can I do? Dan Mason is better than nothing—he amuses me anyway."

"He is not a good man, Lucy, and he will bring you trouble. And please, for my sake, dear, don't disobey your father. You know how terrible he is when he is angry."

"Bah! I'll run away if he ever licks me again—old Terror!"

"Don't Lucy," was all poor Mrs. Lyndon could say, as— sighing heavily, she bent over her work again.

III

The Sacred Institution
of Marriage

One Saturday forenoon Mr. Lyndon came home from work, a very unusual and startling thing for him to do.

"Martha," he said hurriedly, "Squire Thurby is dead and is to be buried over in Neville today and we must go to the funeral. Drop everything and get ready and I'll go get a rig. It will never do for us to stay away from the funeral of such a prominent man and good brother in the church. Now I don't want any everlasting waiting for you to get ready either."

"But James I have set bread and there's nothing ready for the children's dinner—"

"There, no excuses, do as I say. If I ever am able to take you out anywhere you will object of course. You be ready in just half an hour."

Mrs. Lyndon said nothing more. She had to give Lucy instructions about the bread and contrive something for the noonday lunch; tell Hagar how to feed and care for the baby; get her husband's clean shirt and stockings and best suit ready at his hand, then wash and dress herself while haunted with many doubts as to the whereabouts of gloves, best shoes and breastpin, and the consciousness of a rip in her one good dress. She fairly flew about and grew nervous and flushed in her endeavor to be ready in time. But with the girl's help there was only a glove to fasten and a veil to tie on by the time Mr. Lyndon, who had dressed leisurely, called out:

"Now how long have I got to wait for you to primp? I never knew a woman to be ready on time in my life."

They drove away and the children shut the door with a delightful sense of novelty and responsibility. They divided the work between them and performed it with surprising zeal and skill; prepared their lunch and ate it, got baby to sleep, and then found time begin to drag. At this juncture Lucy espied Dan Mason sauntering carelessly by on the opposite side of the street pretending not to notice the house but with eyes very much askant. Lucy tapped on the window; Dan looked around much astonished and seemed disposed to run away, but finally crossed over at Lucy's vehement beckoning. Lucy raised the sash.

"Come in, Dan, for a little while. Father and mother are both gone and we are lonesome. They won't know it."

Lucy had donned her best dress, a dark red merino, when the work was done, had combed her dark hair into soft, wavy half-curls and knew she was looking her best. Dan, only too ready, bounded up the steps and was quickly in the room giving Lucy first an admiring glance then a boisterous kiss. Hagar looked troubled.

"Hallo, little one you look like an actress in a tragedy. What's the matter?"

"I don't think you ought to be here. I wish you would go away. You know father doesn't allow it and it makes mother so much trouble."

"Not if she doesn't know it. Don't you fret. Let's enjoy ourselves. I've got a new book for you and a top and jack knife for you kids an' I'll show you how to make a kite. And let's pop corn or make some molasses candy—oh I know how to play when the old cat's away."

The big hearty, coarse fellow put new life into the children, always so repressed and curbed they hardly knew what fun was. Hagar found the book only a sensational novel of the reddest type but at that age she eagerly devoured everything readable and soon forgot her anxiety in its enticing pages; the others popped corn and played games, laughed and shouted to their heart's content and at last tired out sat around the table and listened to Dan tell wonderful blood curdling stories. Hagar made one of the listeners and even baby was astonishingly good sitting in her lap and staring with round interested eyes at the new face. Dan had Lucy at his side with an arm openly thrown around her. Presently he had no more stories to tell and the children slipped away to amusements of their own; then he began to talk in low tones to her alone. Slowly her head drooped until it rested on his shoulder; her cheeks grew crimson and her long lashes fell languidly over her burning eyes. Time and duty and the outside world were forgotten.

Suddenly Hagar looked up from the book she had resumed—realizing that it had grown too dark to see the words. An ominous chill seized her. What if their father should catch Dan there? And then as if in verification of her fears Bennie cried out, "Here come father and mother!"

Lacy and Dan sprang up startled and dismayed. They could not instantly recall themselves to the realities and seemed lost as to what they should do.

"Dan go quick or father will kill you!" exclaimed Hagar in a suppressed voice.

Now there was nothing in the world to prevent Dan's walking out of the back door across the lot and out to the side street without being seen by Mr. Lyndon; but he was frightened and confused and he was yet under the spell of Lucy's presence. With a vague idea of hiding and taking Lucy with him, he opened the door nearest him which happened to lead into a small bedroom, the one occupied by Hagar and one of the smaller children. He drew the bewildered girl into the room and closed the door. Hagar cried out a quick remonstrance but it was too late—her father entered the room.

There was no cry of welcome from the children; they all stood about in dismayed embarrassment.

"Well what is the matter with you all?" Mr. Lyndon demanded sternly while Mrs. Lyndon hastened to take her baby and examine him closely to see that he was still whole and had not changed beyond recognition. "You look as though you had been into mischief of some kind," he continued. "Where's Lucy?"

No one answered. Hagar drew nearer her mother.

"Where has that girl gone, Hagar?"

"I can't tell you father."

"Do you mean that you don't know?"

"I know but I can't tell."

"What! Do you dare—but I'll attend to you later. Is she in the house?"

No answer from Hagar but the smallest boy besides the baby piped out a shrill "yes sir."

He hurriedly lighted a lamp and looked into the front room or 'parlor,' into his own chamber, in closet and store-room and finally came to the small bedroom door. It was locked. With a violent push he broke the lock and threw the door wide open. Lucy stood before him flushed, startled, disheveled with that spell of languorous loveliness still lingering over her face. Dan stood further back looking sheepish but doggedly defiant.

The situation was too appalling. Of what use were wrath, punishments, the righteous indignation of outraged authority in a case like this? Glaring wickedness such as this going on in the house of a respectable and virtuous church member? He retreated, unable to speak. Dan slouched out with his hands in his pockets carrying a great assumption of carelessness.

"Come, come old man there's no harm done. If you never say anything about it, it's all right—I'm sure I won't. Keep your temper and I'll go."

"Stop! You rascal! Stay where you are. And you, you hussy! How dare you look me in the face?" He had recovered his voice with terrific force and the young couple were awed at his mien and manner.

"I haven't done anything so very bad," said Lucy beginning to cry. "I only called Dan into the house this afternoon because we were so lonesome——"

"Nothing so very bad! Ye gods! Is my child lost to all sense of decency? I find you in a situation that *nothing* can excuse but the fact of your being married and you call it "nothing so very bad." Or perhaps you have disobeyed me before and are already man and wife?"

"Why, of course not father," Lucy hastened to say.

"Then you shall be this very day!" Lyndon roared bringing his fist down on the table with such force that everything in the room shook or jingled. Mrs. Lyndon started up with a cry of dismay. Lucy began to sob and Dan looked frightened.

"I'll not lose sight of you until you are legally married. No daughter of mine shall be found shut up in a bedroom with a man and ever go out of my house a single woman." There was a short pause as though some wandering thought of tenderness or pity had touched him; it was but a moment and his face hardened again.

"Benjamin go over to Rev. Gorman's and tell him I wish him to come here as soon as he possibly can. Say simply this and nothing more."

"I would never have given my daughter to you," he said turning to Dan, "and full well you know it. But she has made it impossible to make any other disposal of her life. She must marry you now."

"But father," sobbed Lucy, "I don't want to marry Dan Mason. I don't want to marry anybody—I'm only a little girl. I won't marry him, I can't father."

"You shall marry him or walk out into the street a disgraced and homeless outcast." James Lyndon was very pale now and his boisterous anger seemed gone, but his face was set and firm as a rock.

"Supposing I refuse?" said Dan.

"You will not refuse. You know when you are well off."

Dan tried to meet the hard, threatening gaze of Lucy's father with as steady a one but failed, and with a shrug of the shoulder said,

"Oh, I'm willing enough. Only you happen to know, I suppose, that I've got precious little to live on."

"I will not send my daughter out penniless. But you must work for your living as better people are obliged to do."

"I don't want to be married! I don't want to be married," Lucy kept saying, crying like a child with her face in her hands as she had done but yesterday over a broken plate.

Mrs. Lyndon came up and put her hand on her husband's arm.

"James you do not mean this, surely?"

"Am I in the habit of saying what I do not mean?"

"But just think—it will affect her whole life and she is but a child. Don't force her into a step that may make her wretched all her days. Don't let us thrust our first born out from our home like this—surely a little imprudence in one so young can be lived down."

"She is too old for it to be 'a little imprudence.' She has disobeyed and defied me. I don't know that she will not keep on doing so, and as she has determined to meet him in spite of me, let her take him now and get enough of him. Come, I've had enough of this. Lucy dry your eyes and make yourself presentable. No scenes now, before the minister, or, I say it—you go out of this house to-night never to enter it again."

"Now I jest want to say Lyndon," began Dan with some sense of justice struggling up through his coarse nature, "that though I'm right fond o' Lucy and willing to get so goodlookin' a wife, she's jest as good a girl for all o' me as she ever was in her life."

"That's what you say; but she is compromised and there is but one way to right the wrong."

Dan went to Lucy and put an arm about her. "Come old girl, you oughtn't to cry so at getting a husband a little sooner than you expected. I'll not be bad to you, and, come now—there's no getting out of it you know."

Lucy looked up and dried her eyes. Dan's personal magnetism swayed her and then she glanced out of the window, saw that it was beginning to snow and heard the wind moan dolefully about the house. Out in the streets on such a night? She shivered, turned, and gave Dan her hand.

A highly respectable and solemn looking man entered. It was the Rev. Gorman who held Brother Lyndon in great esteem because he was one of his chief supporters, and such a shining example of his teaching. Through his habitual solemnity and grave decorum, a gleam of wonder and curiosity struggled which scarcely lessened when Mr. Lyndon explained that a union had been arranged between his daughter and Daniel Mason and for family reasons it had been decided to have the ceremony performed privately and at once. The preacher was obsequiously anxious to please his influential parishioner, and slowly assented but looking perplexed and as though he would like further explanation. None were given however, and the preacher privately determined that he would have it out of Lyndon some day. Now he would do his bidding.

It was a strange wedding. The young bride and groom looked more sullen than happy; the father looked on with stern and gloomy face and the children stood about wondering and frightened. The mother sat, half starting up as though she would arise and forbid the marriage, her face pale and set in a look almost of terror. But she did not speak, and when the minister pronounced them man and wife and proceeded with a prayer, she leaned back with a low, long drawn sob and covered her face.

The common duties of life break in on the most momentous and solemn occasions. Supper was to get ready, evening work to be done, many things to be seen to; they had to eat and speak and meet one another's glances as though nothing had occurred. Even some little effort at gaiety was made at the table, but it was a sorry effort.

"Take your wife home, Daniel," said Lyndon after prayers.

"Oh no, father, let me stay with mother to-night."

"Let me have her my own little girl one night more," pleaded his wife.

Dan stammered and fumbled with his hat, "I'll have to break it to the old folks and fix up a place for her first, I guess." Lyndon for once yielded. "Do as you please," and turned away.

IV

Thy Desire Shall Be unto Thy Husband and He Shall Rule over Thee

A sultry day was just closing some three years after Lucy's impromptu wedding. The long village street rested in the shadows like something wearied with the day's heat and turmoil, pausing to welcome the first fresh coolness of evening. All day, people had gone up and down its busy length, with glowing countenances; steaming horses had drawn loads of hay, wood and vegetables to and fro, and children had played about in the tracks and on the walks and accumulated dust on their sweaty little faces. Later the street would stir again with light footsteps, laughter and the merry voices of youth. The few open shops would throw gleams of light across the dusty road, and the town band would discourse ambitious music from a rickety band stand in the public square. But just now a sweet quiet reigned and a soft breeze was sweeping away the heat and odors of a long, busy, broiling market day. A belated child ran homeward down the walk, a tired shop-keeper wiped his brow in front of his store but otherwise the street was deserted.

In front of the Lyndon cottage a girl of fifteen leaned over the gate holding with one arm a child who was just large enough to sit up on the gatepost. There was always a baby in the Lyndon household; Hagar had shared in the care of two since Johnnie, who was now a sturdy boy, always in the dirt or in disgrace, a great source of anxiety to his patient nurse but very affectionate and warmhearted withal.

Hagar had grown taller but not handsomer. Her face was still thin and sallow, but the large dark eyes with their serious depths, and the delicate, firm mouth rendered it an attractive one, not easily forgotten. She had grown too fast and worked too hard to be graceful and softly rounded; her shoulders drooped, her outlines were angular and she was too slight for beauty. But there existed even now in the over tasked, immature girl promise of a superb womanhood if not too long blighted by poor surroundings. She rested her head wearily on one hand with her face to the breeze, welcoming the coolness that was so great a relief after the heated day. Across a neighboring fence back of their dwellings two women were gossiping. Their sunbonnets swung from their bared arms, the light wind swept their untidy locks into their faces and stirred the folds of their faded cotton dresses. Hagar paid no heed to them until one exclaimed a little louder and clearer than their murmured talk had been,

"Well, I for one don't blame him one bit. What does the woman think? She's married to him, he supports her and she belongs to church and knows her duty.

"Hush! There's Hagar Lyndon standing at their gate. She'll hear you," said the other.

"Oh she never pays no attention to anybody. 'Sides I'd as lief she'd know what I think o' sech things. She's jest the age to have improvin' idees given her."

Hagar might not have noticed the conversation but for hearing her name mentioned; once her attention was attracted it was difficult, as she had good ears, not to hear the remainder of what was said.

"Well I don't think Joe Finley had a right to *beat* her— seems to me a man might get along without pounding his wife. But of course she must expect that, or see him run off with bad women if she won't do as a wife should."

"I'd sooner my man would beat me than do that, but there's no danger of either. I know my duty better. No use in a woman rebellin against the commands of the Bible. She shouldn't enter the holy bonds o' matrimony if she don't want to keep her vows.

But say—don't you think some of us ought to go and see Mrs. Finley? Finley's off buyin' cattle and won't be back before tomorrow night and I hear she's actilly down sick, can't help herself and nobody there but them three young'uns o' hers."

There was a woman coming toward Hagar from the town and she looked wonderingly to see her. The woman was still fresh and young looking, well dressed and smiling, though traces of a hard life of bitterness and sorrow lurked in the attractive and pleasant looking face. Hagar glanced apprehensively back at the windows of the house then seemingly re-assured greeted Clive Daley as she approached.

"Good evening, aunt. Are you staying in Belleville now? I have had several glimpses of you lately."

"Only for a few weeks. I grew so tired of the hot, dusty city and wanted to get away from it all. I like this little town in the summer though I cannot say much for its coolness; and then, I cannot tell why, I like to be near Mattie and you sometimes though I know I must not talk to you. It brings my innocent girlhood back to me.

"But I should think it would be painful, aunt Clive. People slight you and father will not let you visit us."

"I do not mind that any more. I live my own life and think my own thoughts. I would not have lived as I have from choice, but such as I am I would rather be *myself* than many of the women who pull aside their skirts when they meet me. But I do not want to get you into trouble—is your father inside?"

"Yes, up stairs I think."

"Are they all well? As usual; well here is some candy for the little ones and, goodby."

The two gossipers at the fence were silently staring at them. As Miss Daley moved on Hagar heard in a penetrating whisper:

"If Hagar Lyndon ain't actilly talking to that bad aunt of hers! Wouldn't Jim Lyndon give her a good lickin' if he knew it?"

"I've a notion to tell him. You can't watch a young girl like that too close."

"Oh never mind; he'll watch her close enough. Isn't it queer that such a nice, hard workin', pious wife and mother as Mrs. Lyndon is should have such a bold, flaunting wicked sister?"

"Yes it is strange; it happens that way in families sometimes. But as I was sayin', shouldn't somebody as a christian duty, go and see Mrs. Finley?"

"Oh 'twould look like interferin' between man and wife and I never do that. I guess he won't let her die. He'll be home tomorrow and she'll have her lesson learned by that time."

Hagar took her baby sister in her arms and hurried into the house. Her mother sat in a low rocking chair with a huge basket of unmended garments at her side. One child was pulling them out over the floor, two others were draping them over four chairs to constitute "a show" and the mother was hastily putting a few last stitches by the fading light, looking worried and pale.

"Mother may I go up the street a few minutes?—I want to go to the Post-office and to the shoemaker's for my shoe."

"If the baby will be good a few minutes, and you will take Neddie and Johnnie with you and be back before it is very dark, you may. Your father is upstairs looking over his accounts and I must straighten up this room before he comes down."

Hagar put the baby in a high chair with a spoon and clothes-pin to play with, caught the next two younger ones, hurriedly washed their faces, found their hats and her own, then started out with them.

A last look at her mother's sad weary face, with the thought of her aunt's as she had just seen it, started a new query in her mind. "I wonder why it is," she thought as she slowly closed the gate, "that aunt Clive looks so much fresher, brighter and younger than poor mother? They say, mother was the prettier when they were girls and she is only five or six years older though she looks fifteen. Mother is the good one—she has always lived as people think women should live but instead of being happier for it she is the saddest person I know. Aunt Clive is bitter and says sharp things sometimes but she seems cheerful and young after all. It is strange that the path of virtue is so very hard."

Just then one of her little charges ran away from her and across the road; a team turned the corner driven at full speed and almost ran over the little fellow. Some one on the opposite walk, the same one Neddie had started to see, sprang into the road and deftly grasped the boy almost from under the horses' feet, and carried him unhurt to Hagar. She was pale but silent, fright froze her into a statue-like quiet, never rousing her into screams.

"You will have to tie strings to this little urchin, Hagar, when you take him out," said the young man as he lifted his hat and brushed back his light brown curls. It was Paul Deane. He had grown handsomer than men ever ought to be—they who monopolize so many advantages should leave beauty to the weaker sex. But, as it was the intelligence of his bright face and the kindness in his ever-ready smile that made up the great charm people felt in his presence, rather than regularity of feature and clearness of coloring, his beauty may be forgiven him.

"I can't thank you enough, Paul," Hagar said earnestly. "What would I have done if Ned had got hurt?"

"Oh, what I did was nothing, only I'm glad I was on hand. Warm, isn't it?"

Hagar was not in a mood for talking, so she merely assented, thanked him again and moved on. Paul paused and looked after her wistfully as though he would like to go with her; but he probably knew by experience that it was not best to follow Hagar without express permission and slowly walked away.

The girl hurriedly performed her errands then quickly as the children could walk took her way toward the other end of town and down a narrow side street or lane. In front of a small board house she placed the children on the walk and bribed them to remain perfectly still while she went in. A side door was standing open; two children sat near it on a rug playing with dolls in a subdued way. Low voices drifted out from an inner room. She rapped but no one answered and the little ones only stared in vague wonder. Stepping inside she looked into the next room and saw her aunt bending over a bed where a sick woman lay; the woman was talking in a suppressed voice as if fearful even then that it would be heard where wrath would follow. "Oh you don't know, Miss Daley, how I've suffered; I couldn't help it if it was wicked to refuse him—I couldn't let him kill me. I've borne three children and I'm only married four years. I am in misery all the time and when he came to me last night—"

The voice went on. The cheeks of the young, ignorant girl who stood listening as under a spell, burned with indignation, shame, and the shock of a sudden knowledge of terrible things. She drew back into the shadow.

Her aunt's voice, softened and gentle as she had never heard it, seemed to be uttering soothing words. She heard the clink of a spoon against a glass, the low rustle of pillows and blankets being arranged and knew Clive Daley was doing all that could be done for the sick woman. She could not bear to meet any one just then with those new, strange, shocking words sending the blood surging in hot rushes through her veins. The poor woman was being cared for and she would go, without letting them know of her presence. It was quite dark when she came out; she wondered that the children had not been calling for her, but found them contentedly talking with some one standing on the walk beside them.

"Don't take it amiss, Hagar, that I came round to see that you got home safe. I happened to see you turn down here as I was on my way home and it looks lonesome down this way—I thought I would wait for you."

It was Paule Deane's voice, and Hagar felt a little impatient for she wished to talk to no one just then. She only murmured an inaudible reply.

"This little one is sleepy; I'll carry him, and you Johnnie, stick to your sister for I couldn't grab you quick enough to get you out of danger now. I didn't know, Hagar, that you were

acquainted with the Finleys. Joe is a rough chap—I don't fancy
him, but his wife seems like a nice little woman enough—sickly
looking though."

"She is sick and all alone. I never spoke to her in my life,
but when I heard she was alone and suffering I wanted to see if I
could do anything for her. I am not needed however—aunt Clive
is there."

"Is Clive Daley there? Are you yet friendly to her? I know
your father and mother do not speak to her."

"Yes, my aunt Clive is there, caring for a poor, sick, abused
woman when not a church-member in town will go near her. You
always see aunt Clive where she can do good and other women
with their piety where they can sting some one, or crush out
all the natural joy there is in people. I am getting tired of the
solemn, miserable, hypocritical cant they call religion."

"I haven't much use for it myself. I never saw that it had
much effect on people except to make them stern and miserable.
But then I think it right that respectable women and girls
should keep themselves separate from those who are considered
disreputable."

"I don't know," answered Hagar slowly. "It seems to me if
a woman who is 'considered disreputable' does more real good
than respectable people, she is far more worthy. Now aunt Clive
is called a bad woman and father will not allow me to speak to

her. Yet she is always helping some one. Last month when she was at home, she found a poor railroad hand's wife sick, five children down with the measles, and baby twins by her side. One or two church women had called, but the filth and disorder frightened them. Aunt Clive went there, rolled up her sleeves, cleaned them all up—rooms, bed, mother and children, down to the twins. She nursed them two days and nights, then went to the deacons of the church and shamed them into getting up a subscription and hiring a nurse. I've known her to do other such deeds—not as charity, but as one friend would go to another.

"All the wives and mothers who are 'poor but respectable' seem so careworn and unhappy. Aunt Clive is fresh looking and cheerful as ever, though she has a certain gravity about her, and a serious way of studying people."

"Miss Daley does seem good-natured and kind. I don't know as I ever thought before how good a woman, a disgraced one, might be. Where do you get your odd, original way of looking at things, Hagar? Every one around you is conventional enough."

"I don't know. I get so tired of people with their strict codes that seem all awry with the real nature of things. I believe whatever makes people happy is right and all that creates misery is wicked. But that is opposed to every article of the creed."

"I believe you are right. I take home something to think of every time I see you, and that is why I'd rather talk to you than any girl in town."

"Oh hurry—pa has come down and is scolding about me. Give me Neddie and—don't come in, Paul, or he'll be more angry than ever."

"Is he cross? Will he hurt you? Let me go in and take the blame."

"No, no, that would never do. Goodnight. Johnnie, don't tell pa."

Johnnie was used to keeping things from pa and murmured "No, I won't, Hagie," as the door opened.

Out from the room were borne on the air, the heavy, authoritative tones of a man. "You ought to have more sense than to let that girl go traipsing the streets until after dark. One lesson such as you've had ought to do you. You know your duty as wife and mother well enough, I'll—" the door closed with a slam. From the village square a strain of music arose and filled the air, a laugh rang out and a gurgle of many young voices floated by on the summer night wind. So closely do the gaieties and troubles of life intermingle.

V

The Duties and Pleasures of Wife and Mother

Hagar's sister lived not far from the parent home in a little two

roomed house that had been hastily put up shortly after her

sudden marriage. Her husband drove a team, when not otherwise

occupied, and earned a scanty living that he would have spent

during those otherwise occupied hours, if Lucy had not usually

been too sharp for him. There was not an overabundance of

comfort in the humble home and whenever Mrs. Lyndon could

spare anything from her own store without cognizance of the

head of the house, she quietly sent it to her daughter. Hagar went

on such an errand one sunny afternoon, accompanied by one of the children—it was seldom she could stir from home without assuming charge of one or two. Lucy met her at the door, carrying a year old baby while an older one pulled at her skirts; her hair, no longer trained in soft wavy curls, lay tousled and dusty on her neck, half falling out of a loose knot. Her face, though no longer round and rosy could not as yet be otherwise than pretty, though it had grown hard and fretful looking. Her dress was careless and untidy as was the room into which Hagar entered.

"I'm glad you've come, Hagar. It seems to me you never come unless you must, and I get so tired staying with these young ones every blessed minute of my life."

"Why don't you bring them over home oftener? Or I could stay with them sometimes if you want to go out."

"Oh it's such a task to get myself and the two of them ready just to go over to mother's and I've really no where else to go after all."

"But why not wash and dress yourselves up a little every day anyway? You have plenty of time and would get interested in making the children look pretty. It isn't as though you had something else to occupy your mind and time. I can't see how you've fallen into such careless ways, Lucy; you did not used to be so."

"Don't lecture, sis. I haven't the heart for it and what's the use? I never see any one and even Dan isn't home much and for that matter I'd rather look worse than better for him. I don't care about his being gone so much only that I know he is spending the little money he has at the tavern; when he is here he is either quarrelsome, or affectionate as a bear and I get tired of him. I am dreadfully tired of my life any way. Here I am only a young girl and I ought to be going to parties and enjoying myself and having agreeable young men wait on me; instead of that, I am always tied down to this miserable little house with only two mischievous children for company."

To Hagar the whole idea of her sister's being married at all had something so tragical in it that actual complaints from Lucy seemed appalling. There appeared to be no consoling side to look at, and her eyes grew larger and more solemn, as was their wont when she was troubled. What could be said or done to help her sister bear her burdens?

Hagar had no religious consolation to offer. She had heard so much of the cant dealt out where something practical was needed, so much advice as to "patience" and "going to the Lord with one's sorrows" when no such process could give any relief, that she had no faith in any of it. She could see no redeeming feature in her sister's bondage. She was slow to comprehend a feeling she had never experienced and she had seen so little of conjugal love manifested, she hardly understood what the motive was supposed to be that induced young men and women to leave home and comparative freedom, to tie themselves down to poverty, monotony and hard work. All the wives she knew were weary, faded and meek, or silly, gossiping and deceitful; the husbands, creatures to be conciliated and avoided as much as possible. She could not perceive that Dan's fitful, half-savage, jealous sort of love for Lucy or her impatient, willful endurance of his caresses, had any elements of happiness in them. Children seemed the only possible consolation in such a life, and if they failed—well, there was none!

"But the children are company for you, aren't they?" she said at length. "They are sweet and lovable and you find some pleasure in them for I know you are fond of them."

"Oh of course Kittie and Frankie are dear little things but one would grow tired of Heaven if tied up with a chain that never gives way. I like my children but I can't always be wrapt up in them alone. Married women are supposed to need nothing on earth but the company of their children and I don't see why; I wish I could get away from them sometimes."

"Oh Lucy if you feel that way, I don't know what on earth to do. If your babies don't comfort you, there is nothing but patient endurance for you the same as for all other women."

"Oh bother! I don't mean to be a bit patient. I mean to scold and get what I want. I believe I'll run away and ask aunt

Clive to take me to the city with her. I'll do that or get religion and join the church—there would be some excitement in that."

"You would only be miserable unless you were really in earnest. If there is really no way out of it, you can't better matters by keeping in a turmoil."

"I like turmoil better than stagnation. Wait until you are married then you will know how I feel."

"I never will marry, Lucy. Nothing on earth could make me. If it had been me, father tried to force into a marriage, I should have run out into the storm and wandered about till I died."

"Oh! you don't know what you would have done, you solemn little innocent. Wait till Paul Deane asks you to be his wife and you will tell a different story."

A quick flush swept over Hagar's cheeks but a frightened, troubled look stole into the dark eyes immediately.

"Oh, I hope he will never, never think of such a thing. We are such good friends and I like him so well that it would be terrible to spoil all our pleasure in one another's company, with any such thoughts. No, I don't *believe* Paul will ever want to marry me," Hagar went on indignantly as though she had been accused of harboring disgraceful motives, "I can't imagine him *anybody's* husband."

Lucy laughed rather mockingly and pulled one of the children away from the stovehearth where it was industriously strewing ashes over the floor. Some one knocked at the door. Lucy gave her hair a quick brush, threw off a soiled apron and flung a pink scarf around her collarless neck. Their conversation had given her face a brightness and glow which the scarf set off, and without knowing it, she was looking particularly well as she opened the door. A young stranger, stylish, handsome and debonair, evidently not an inhabitant of their town, stood on the steps. He had not been looking to see a pretty young woman open the door, and he touched his hat with a bright smile as his eyes met Lucy's.

"Good afternoon, Miss, and pardon me for intruding, but can I see your father or—or the good man of the house? I understood a Mr. Mason, a teamster, lived here."

"Mr. Mason does live here but he is not in at present," Lucy answered flutteringly, for the stranger and his words and an embarrassing sense of not being very tidy, confused her.

Thereupon the stranger nonchalantly leaned against the casement and began to explain volubly how he had found himself at the depot with a lot of sample trunks, and something wrong with the hotel team and a great necessity for getting said trunks where he could unpack immediately and, was it likely he could procure the services of her father very soon?

Lucy blushingly replied, "Mr. Mason is my husband not my father, and you will probably find him on the street somewhere."

"It isn't possible? I supposed I was speaking to a young girl just out of school. I beg your pardon, I am sure, for my very natural mistake," and in a suave, easy manner the stranger continued to "make talk" and gaze at Lucy's bright eyes, with roving glances for Hagar and the children, through several minutes. Finally, when he could conjure up nothing more to linger and talk about, he stepped backward, a little to the side, bowing and smiling, with his hat in his hand, and so doing, crushed a little rose plant that grew by the door. Most profuse was he in apologies and regrets and ended by asking to be allowed to send one the of choicest plants to be found, in the place of it.

Hagar had not spoken, and indeed the stranger had scarcely noticed her plain serious face; she was glad he had not, for something about the man repulsed her. She instinctively felt indignant at the warm, bold glances he gave her sister, though she scarcely knew why she should, and experienced a vague relief when he was finally gone. Lucy had gone to the glass to see how she looked.

"Will you go home with me, Lucy?" Hagar asked.

"Oh no—not today. I don't feel equal to it. I have a novel to read and I am going to take it easy the rest of the day. Oh, you remember we were talking about Paul Deane just as that man interrupted. Well, I only wanted to say, dear, that you will do well to get as good a husband as he will make, and I would advise you to be careful how you use him."

"I don't want you to talk of him in that way, Lucy. I was in earnest in what I said."

"And—say—don't think I meant what I said about being reckless and running away. I am not so wicked as that, after all."

"But will you still be so miserable? If there is no redeeming feature in your life—let us run away from it all, and I will help you to commence life over again."

"Leave my husband? Oh you disgraceful girl, to want me do such a disreputable thing! Oh no—don't worry about me—run along and think I am doing very well. When Dan comes we shall quarrel a little and make it up and commence again tomorrow morning. Nobody else can change it—that is—no, nobody can."

Hagar called her little brother and walked slowly home. The older she grew the more she saw to sadden and weigh her down. Every relation she held toward other people but tended to foster that strong rebellious tendency and the deep determination in her character that in after life led her through her strange course.

VI

When There's Love at Home

Much of the little enjoyment that entered into Hagar's life sprang

from the companionship of her boyish friend Paul Deane. She

never thought of him as a lover, and the few times she heard

him mentioned as a possible husband had made her shudder.

Their friendship was so natural and open, it was more like the

comradeship of two boys than the romantic attachment of girl

and boy. Paul was an only child, the son of a happy mother

and a good father; this it was that made him truthful, candid,

thoughtful—quick to comprehend Hagar's half-formed original

ideas—ready to sympathise with her sad moods and vague

discontent. Mr. Lyndon seldom interfered, though his orders as to "traipsing the streets after dark" were as strict as ever. He rather approved of Paul as a possible match since Mr. Deane was well-to-do and the young man himself was steady and promising—not quite punctual enough in his attendance at church perhaps, but more free than usual of the commoner vices. Sometimes Paul spent rather a dull evening with the family, where the repression and strict order cast a gloom over everything; but their greatest pleasure was in the walks of early mornings or evenings and sometimes in the afternoons when Paul was not busy in the little country printing office. If Hagar took charge of two or three of the children and was in the house before absolute darkness fell, no one objected to her walks. As love never formed the topic of conversation, she felt frank and free; the enjoyment of them, the exercise, the fresh air, combined to make her happier and healthier than she would otherwise have been.

Paul, from the ordinary, properly behaved and rather conservative young man he was naturally inclined to be, was growing more into Hagar's ways of thinking, and ceased to be surprised at her odd thoughts and queer little sayings. In practical information, in literature and science, he was teacher in their talks; in originating new trains of thought, in imaginative and speculative realms, she was leader, and each benefited the other.

They were passing Lucy's house one day, leading the inevitable children, just when the sunset skies were changing to a purplish gray with touches of deep crimson here and there. A rare rose plant stood on the ledge of the front window, bearing a cluster of roses in full bloom that greatly beautified the dull little house. Lucy was bending over it, her own cheeks as crimson as the flowers, while there dwelt on her unusually bright eyes a strange and conscious look.

"Oh how lovely!" exclaimed Hagar pausing at the gate. "Where did you get it?"

"They are rather pretty aren't they? The plant was sent to replace one that was destroyed—not exactly destroyed but hurt"—for the original bush thrust its small branches out as obtrusively as ever in its place, scarcely affected by one careless footstep.

Hagar looked troubled. She was really glad to see Lucy look so bright and interested; she would be pleased if her sister should make new friends or meet with pleasant incidents that might break the wearisomeness of her life and bring back some of the old time freshness and sprightliness into her fast-fading face. But her intuitions were quick and she divined trouble. Dan would object she knew, and he was an untamed devil when his passions were roused.

"I am glad you have them to look at. May I have one?"

"And may I?" asked Paul smiling, and no one could resist his smile. "You will have quite a handful left."

Lucy, framed in the little window casing, with her head on one side and a hand poised, pondered which two of the flowers she could spare best; she looked unusually pretty and girlish standing there, for once in a clean gown with her wavy hair nicely brushed and that unusual animation brightening her face. Down the street Dan was coming with swift uneven strides and Hagar knew by his appearance that he was considerably excited either by drink or some unusual occurrence, probably both.

"Halloa, youngsters!" He called out as soon as he was within calling distance. "Why don't you go in? Can't you make old married folks like us a visit once in a while?"

He came up and boisterously shook hands, threw back his hat and looked up at Lucy.

"By George! Ain't I got a handsome wife, Deane? Old Lyndon did me a favor once if he never did again," and the next moment he was in the house giving Lucy a savage hug which she resented with little screams and scratches. Dan's eyes fell on the rose bush.

"Where the devil did that come from?" he demanded.

"Oh, that!" answered Lucy, trying to speak carelessly. "Mr. Harter brought it for one he stepped on and broke."

"Who in h——l is Mr. Harter?"

"The gentleman you hauled some trunks for one day; he came here that day to inquire for you."

"That d——d smirking wax figger? Why, I just met him down the street and took pains to get in his way, for I've been dying to spoil his devilish smooth face for him ever since I first saw it. But the coward wouldn't fight. Why—damn it, he must have just come away from here. He's been here twice! And he dares come foolin' round my wife and bringin' her trumpery poises. Why——" and he broke into a string of oaths, which it is not worth wasting italics and dashes to designate, and ended by kicking the flower pot out into the yard. The young people still stood at the gate doubtful what to do. Hagar wanted to hasten as far away from Dan as possible, but she feared for Lucy's safety while he was in such a passion, as well she might. Paul, much embarrassed, awaited her motions.

"Dan, you're a brute!" exclaimed Lucy as she ran out and tenderly lifted the broken jar. This maddened Dan; he was scarcely himself anyway, and Lucy's defiance in caring so much for the flowers acted upon his jealous passion like oil upon fire. He ran and grabbed the plant from her and flung it as far into the street as he could send it. She struck at him with impotent fury and he, in his rage, first shook her as a terrier would a rat, then gave her a blow that laid her senseless at his feet. Paul sprang for him, and Hagar flew to her sister's side; but Dan, instantly sobered at seeing Lucy lying white-faced and cold on the ground, shook off the young man as though he were a child, pushed

Hagar aside and gathered his unconscious young wife up in his arms.

"My God! I've killed her! But she's mine, she's mine. Nobody shall interfere—nobody else shall have her. She's mine I tell you. What if I did strike her? I'd do it again and then love her back to life."

He carried her into the house and sat down upon the lounge, still holding her and swayed back and forth or pausing to press her fiercely to his breast, talking wildly all the time. All four of the children were crying with fright; Lucy's face looked death-like and Dan seemed beside himself. Hagar was trembling so violently she could scarcely stand, but she firmly controlled herself and set about looking for something to bring her sister to consciousness. She found some camphor, Paul brought water and between them they made Dan understand that something must be done for Lucy or she would die. They spoke of sending for a doctor but concluded to try all means possible and keep the unfortunate affair to themselves. Both worked so faithfully that presently a long shuddering sigh and a quivering of the eyelids denoted that life was returning. They waited only long enough to see that the poor girl was out of danger, to quiet her two children, to caution Dan about the care of his wife, then hastened on their way. Hagar was uneasy lest her father should have missed her, and could scarce restrain her pace to the capacity of her little brothers.

"I don't want to tell them at home what has happened. Father will blame Lucy and mother will look so grieved and frightened. I'll simply say I was delayed and take a scolding—I think it will be no worse. Isn't it all terrible, Paul? Think of Lucy—so young with such a long life like that before her. I cannot see how any young girl can voluntarily enter into such a stage as marriage seems to be. And yet, all the girls I know appear to be looking forward to marriage as the one aim of their lives. I cannot understand it."

"All marriages are not like Dan and Lucy's," said Paul gently.

"No—some are worse," Hagar continued, unconsciously reversing his meaning. "Dan loves Lucy and I know women seem to think *that* a great consideration. His very love is a terror to her. It makes him savage, jealous, tyrannical and brutal. Marriage must be easier to endure without love, it seems to me."

"But all husbands are not like Dan Mason, and all love is not like his," again suggested Paul.

"Husbands as a class are sure to be disagreeable in one way or another; good men are never husbands."

"What a sweeping assertion! *My* father is a good man."

"He is an exception, and he would be kind in any position. I cannot reconcile his goodness with his willingness to make a good woman his wife, however."

"I think, dear Hagar, you are too extreme on this subject. You are much too bitter for so young a girl—what has made you so?"

"All I see about me—my mother's life, my sister's, my neighbors'. I will tell you more some day for we are nearly home now. Thank you, Paul, for you kindness to-night.

Paul bade her goodnight a little sadly and walked slowly and thoughtfully away.

Lucy seemed as well as usual when next Hagar saw her; she made but one reference to the trouble of that evening, then spoke of other things indifferently and altogether seemed dreamy and less talkative than usual. Dan had begged her forgiveness, she said, and nearly hugged her to death; but he would use her so again if he got in a rage. "But bother!" she dismissed the subject with, "I don't care. He's got a job that keeps him away from home most of the time now, and I'm glad of it."

More than once during the weeks that followed, Hagar was quite sure she saw Lucy lingering under the trees that shaded the walks near her house, just at dusk and though she did not plainly discern another form, felt certain she was not alone. Once she met her and the gentleman she had called Mr. Harter, face to face; it was still daylight and they seemed to be walking in from the country. Hagar bowed and smiled faintly and walked quietly away.

"That means more trouble," she thought, "but poor Lucy! if she had not all her life been constantly kept away from pleasant society she would not steal out to find it in this way. If this man could come openly and naturally to the house and visit the family I don't believe any harm would come of it. For I don't like the man and Lucy would soon see that he is shallow and conceited. Now she is dazzled and—oh dear, I dread the outcome."

So, Hagar had much to trouble her. Her mother's strength seemed waning; she was so very still and white, so patient under the prospective new burden that awaited her that Hagar, looking at her, trembled with an undefined dread. The children were troublesome and rebellious, requiring all her tact and ingenuity to keep them from worrying mother and angering father. They were quiet enough when he was about, but if he discovered delinquencies committed in his absence punishment fell as though he had been present. Hers were not the romantic sorrows young girls often love to cherish, but commonplace, wearing troubles that crush out youthful brightness and turn girlhood too early into serious, stern womanhood.

The days went on and Hagar saw no more of the stranger. But one afternoon Lucy ran over hurriedly and seemed in an unusual mood. She apparently tried to be natural but she kissed her mother when she left with tears in her dark eyes; Hagar was haunted by her unusual demonstration of feeling and later found reason for further misgiving. The children were playing with a little pink, glossy bit of paper they had found and finally began to quarrel over it. Hagar took it from them. The quality and perfume about it attracted her attention; she opened it and read the clear masculine writing upon it.

"Lucy: come to the train at the last moment

from the opposite side to that on which the depot

stands. No one will see you. Everything satisfactorily

arranged. Destroy this: H.H."

What was she to do? Could she prevent this mischief? When, where, how was is to be done? Was is her business? A thousand thoughts and queries surged through her brain as she stood grasping the portentous scrap of paper in her hand. A moan and a low cry from her mother aroused her. She was lying back in her chair insensible. Then all else was forgotten.

VII

God's Will Be Done

A stormy evening was drawing on. Hagar, pale and sorrowful,
gathered the children around her endeavoring to keep them quiet.
The mother's low chair was vacant—the homely sitting-room was
empty of her presence. With varied anxieties wearing her soul
Hagar sat near the window thinking she might get one glimpse
of Lucy, and resolving to run out and stop her if she should, at
any risk; she dared not ask permission to leave for even a short
time—it would have been useless and would have seemed strange.
And so, while the darkness gathered and the storm rose she kept
at her post. A heavy important-looking woman passed in and out
of an adjoining apartment, with bottles, basins and aired sheets

in her hands. Two doctors were in attendance, and when the door opened, low moans pierced the heart of the anxious daughter.

The children were one by one sent to bed. All night long, while the thunder rumbled and muttered and the rain poured on the roof and was swept by the wind in heavy sheets against the windows, the moans of mortal agony continued. The nurse went to and fro with stolid face, the father lay on a lounge gloomily waiting and listening.

Toward morning silence fell. The storm rumbled itself off out of hearing, the moans had died away, and the nurse's steps had ceased. Under the light of a few pale stars that peeped out from the clouds but to be quenched by the dawn, the two doctors rode away. Their work was done, and however it had ended, they looked forward to rest. Hagar lying awake up stairs in her little bed where she had been ordered many hours before, wondered what had happened. Was all well? She longed to creep down and see but it was yet too early and she did not dare. With the first ray of the sun across her room she was up and dressed.

"May I come in?" she softly questioned at her mother's bedroom door.

Some one slowly opened it. Her father sat at the foot of the bed, with his head bowed in his hands; the woman was putting the room to rights in a business like manner. A sheet was drawn over her mother's face—with a sharp, quick, chill at her heart Hagar went up to the bed and turned it down.

The still, cold, thin face of her mother met her gaze—peaceful and free from any look of suffering, as she had not seen it for years. On her bosom lay a little dead baby. For many moments—awful, silent, dragging moments, Hagar looked at that calm face, then stooped and pressed a kiss on the white lips and reverently covered it. There were no tears in her eyes.

"Hagar, God has seen fit to remove your mother. Do you feel no grief at her departure?"

Her father who had raised his head when she entered the room and watched with a stern surprise, spoke in low awe-struck tones.

"My mother is not suffering any more. I cannot cry to have her back again where she was never without pain, never happy. If it was God's will to remove her it was because He was powerless to help her any other way."

For a moment the father look shocked; then he piously murmured "Whom the Lord loveth he chasteneth," and bowed his head upon his hands again.

Hagar left the room and went out to look upon the newly-washed earth where a million drops of water glistened under the long slant rays of the morning sun.

"Why did not God save her all that suffering if he has so much power? 'Saw fit to remove her,' indeed! She died because she had endured just all she could. She never, never more would have been free from pain. I am glad"—slowly and solemnly she said it—"I am glad she is at rest."

———————

That night had brought storm and pain to humanity, while it lashed the elements into a frenzy. Early in the evening, when the first great black clouds came rolling up over the blue dome, Lucy sat in her little home, her elder child clasped closely in her arms, her baby asleep in its cradle. She seemed strangely excited and her moods varied with the rising and falling of the storm; one moment she would put down the child and hurriedly begin to gather up a few of her small belongings; then a glance at the baby or the voice of her boy would check her and she would take the child again and sit quietly down. A fiercer gust of wind than usual would arouse her once more. Again she would begin preparations for a journey and again her children seemed to draw her back. At last both children were sound asleep and she laid them, in clean white gowns, side by side in her own bed. The rain was falling heavily now, while the thunder's roar and lightning's flash made of the heavens an imaginary battlefield. Inside, the little house was very gloomy for the one lamp burned dimly and the shadows fell darkly over the bare uneven floor, the wooden chairs and rough table. Lucy sat with her head leaned on the window sill, scarcely moving while nearly an hour of storm and darkness went by. Then she rose determinedly.

"I'll go. I am so tired of it all. I've had no chance—no pleasures—I won't bear it. Dan is as rough when he loves me as when he is angry and he hurts me either way. He and Hagar won't let the children suffer and what else need I care for. I will not stay here any longer, but Harter is mistaken if he thinks—" Some sound startled her and she paused; but presently reassured, she went on with her preparations. "Dan will be home a little after nine. The train does not come till nearly ten but he will not find me in that short time. Now for freedom! They'll find they can't tie down a young girl like me to such a life. But—" she paused again.

"I will be disgraced. I am doing the thing I told Hagar I never would do. I can never be a respectable woman again.

"I can't help it. Something is drawing me on. I can't stay here." She wrapped a long dark cloak around her, put on a small hat and a heavy veil over it; turned the light lower and went out into the terrific storm. At first she could not keep her feet for the rain and wind, but by dint of scurrying along when there was a lull and crouching close to the fence when the blasts came too strong, she managed to make headway. The night was so black except when turned to a vivid glare by the lightning, that she could no more see than if she had been totally blind. To go to the opposite side of the depot she was obliged to traverse a long lonely street and walk around a great line of freight cars standing on a side track. Every step was a struggle. Sometimes she stepped off the walk and stumbled about in dripping weeds and grass a long time before she found the right path again. But at last, half-drowned, panting and trembling, she reached a spot where she could see the light of the depot throw cheerful gleams across the tracks where the projecting roof of an old freight house sheltered her from the worst fury of the storm, and where she could not be seen had any one been about. And there in the darkness, with that wild glare turning the world into sulphuric day one moment, and leaving it in thick blackness the next amid the crash and rumble of thunder, the shrieking of the wind and the ceaseless splash of the rain, Lucy waited—it seemed to her, an eternity. No train, no footsteps on the platform, no official's lantern, it was as though the living world she was accustomed to had vanished, and chaos had come instead.

At last the far off town clock boomed out the hour of twelve—she had somehow missed eleven in the noise of battling elements—and the sound brought her back to the realities again. Everything was as it always had been, after all. A heavy footstep sounded at the farther end of the platform—a hurried angry step that she knew full well. She saw a big burly form outlined against the depot window for one moment; then there came a light springing step from the same direction that sent the blood rushing to her cheeks and away again, leaving them white and cold. A natty figure well shielded from the storm came into the small spot of light. There was a sound of voices in dispute—gruff, raging tones mingled with a smooth, penetrating voice, then a blow—a moment's silence and a pistol shot rang out.

Lucy started. "He has killed him! He will kill me if he finds me here. Oh where shall I hide?"

With but the thought that she must fly for safety she ran from the depot out toward an open field; a fence crossed her way which she clambered over as best she could; then on and on, over wet grass, ditches, bushes, stumps, in perfect darkness and torrents of rain, she flew until completely exhausted. She fell at last at the foot of a tree where the grass was thick and soft. Sitting there, her pulses wildly beating, struggling for breath and with queer lights dancing before her eyes, she heard the whistle of the belated train far away. It rushed into the depot, paused but a moment, panting and clanging its hurrying bell, then tore away into the distance. It was not carrying her away as she had thought once it would. Who else had it left? Was Harter gone or was he dead? And where was Dan?

The storm was slowly dying away. The far away flickerings of light athwart the sky, did not show Lucy her surroundings. She knew every foot of the ground around the village and as yet, it had not occurred to her to be anxious about her way. She was wet through, cold, and oh! so tired. All the romance, the vague longings to reach something brighter and happier than anything she had ever known, had left her. She thought of her warm bed at home, her pretty babies, the little stove sending out its grateful heat, with intense longing. To sit there dry and warm, the tea kettle singing, the frying pan with a good steak sizzling within it—why that was happiness enough for any one. How silly she had been! She thought she could well endure Dan for the sake of these common comforts after all. She would go home.

Dragging her chilled and stiffened frame upright, she took a few steps forward. But it dawned upon her that she did not know which way to go. The feel of the ground was unfamiliar, a fence came in her way that seemed strangely out of place and not the faintest ray of light came to show her a single land-mark. She could only stumble and grope about in her dripping garments, shivering, aching in every joint, through the long, still hours before the clouds rolled away from placid stars. The first faint pearly rays of dawn showed her her whereabouts—a pasture field a mile or more outside the edge of town. By this time another revulsion of feeling had taken place. Fear of Dan, disgust with her life, a longing for the old home with mother where she could be a child with the other children, came surging over her. She was only a young girl after all—she would go home and let mother put her to bed, and then—how she would sleep! No more a wife and mother—only a sleeping child under her own mother's care. Lucy's tired brain was whirling, nothing was real but her weariness.

Suddenly, out of the vanishing darkness, a form appeared; it was dripping and muddied like her own, its face was haggard and frightened. She did not know how wan and ghost-like she herself looked in her long clinging cloak, or she might have accounted for the look of awe that rested on his face.

"Lucy, is it *you*, alive?"

"Yes it's me—alive. Why not?"

"Then—you little she-devil, ain't you afraid I'll kill you? Where have you been all night?"

"I won't tell you; and I won't stand it to be beaten or shaken, I tell you. Don't you touch me! You never shall touch me again. I'm going home to mother."

Something in her strange, determined manner, her wild white face, awed the man.

"Come home, Lucy," he said more quietly. "Come home and get some dry clothes on. Don't be a fool."

"I'll not go to *your* home any more. Let me alone. You've done a murder—don't come near me!"

Dan did not answer, but strode along after her as she walked feebly toward her old home. Under the glittering trees just as the sun rose, they saw Hagar standing looking up at the sky with that wrapt and solemn expression on her face.

"Hagar, take me home," Lucy said wearily, showing no surprise at meeting her sister out so early.

"Why, Lucy, what is it? How strangely you look! And Dan, too? You have both been out in the storm." Then she remembered the note she had found the night before and kept silent. At least they were both here, unhurt and together.

"I want my mother, Hagar—nobody else can do me any good. Take me to her."

"My poor, poor sister! I know you never wanted your mother as you do just now. But our mother will never soothe our pain or watch over our sleep again. She is dead, Lucy."

Hagar had put both arms about Lucy's cold, wet form before she told her this, but she slipped through the frail support and fell unconscious. It needed but this to finish the work of the long strain and terrible exposure of the night.

"Poor, poor Lucy. How she has suffered!" moaned Hagar bending over her and chafing her cold face.

"Here, let me have her," said Dan savagely stooping and taking her in his powerful arms as easily as Hagar would a little child.

"I'll take care of her. Go back home, Hagar, and say nothing about this. I can nurse her as tenderly as her mother could—you can trust me."

Hagar knew that in his present mood he would, and she let him go.

VIII

A Mysterious Visitation
of Providence

The day of the funeral came. The still, white form of the mother
and wife, robed in a snowy shroud lay at rest in the humble
home that was in the primmest order, decorously darkened and
appropriately stilled. The children sat quietly where they had
been placed, awed and frightened, wondering what strange, sad
thing had happened to mother, while Hagar very pale but with a
glad light in her solemn eyes, hovered near, longing to get them
to herself to talk and comfort, to see them break their unnatural
quiet, and cry and be consoled again. Neighbors had taken
possession of the house; they moved officiously about the rooms,

making their ostentatious stillness and mournful importance
manifest in many a creaking footstep and penetrating whisper.
Her father kept in his own apartment and she only heard his
voice when some one asked a question for directions.

In her own home Lucy lay raving in a fever. One or two
women had gone in to help, but Dan would not let them come
near his wife—he had no mind to let them hear her mutterings
about going away, her cries for her mother, the angry supplicating
or frightened words to him which burdened her delirium. She
whispered another name sometimes that brought a fierce light in
his eyes and an ugly scowl on his face, but the sad, weary words
that quickly followed allayed his wild emotion. The neighbors
took the children home and left him alone with his sick wife and
for many days and nights he watched over her.

"She takes it terr'ble hard—her mother's death," the
neighbors said, and never guessed that anything had gone before
it.

Some way Clive Daley heard of her sister's death, and on
the morning of the day she was to be buried, arrived in town and
came to the door of the house of mourning. The startled neighbor
who opened the door did not know what to say, but she was quite
sure she ought not to set foot within that virtuous home; so she
sent another woman to ask Mr. Lyndon what she should do. Tears
were in Miss Daley's softened eyes as she said:—

"It surely can't hurt any one if I come in and look on the dead face of my poor sister, that I could not see alive. I might comfort Hagar and the children—don't be alarmed that I shall remain and annoy any one long."

"Mr. Lyndon says you cannot come in; that you should be ashamed to offer to come, and that you are by no means to speak to Hagar or any of the children," haughtily announced the woman who had gone on the errand. Miss Daley drew her rich shawl closer about her, bowed, and walked proudly away.

But they could not keep her from coming to the church where the services were held. She sat where she could look at Hagar, and when the young girl's eyes fell on the sympathetic face of her aunt, they brightened as nothing any one else had looked or done or said to her, could brighten them. Aunt Clive might be very wicked but there was something in her eyes that seemed to meet her own embittered soul in sympathy, to say that she was understood, to soften the hard, cold feeling dwelling within her bosom toward all the world.

With all the ceremonies of the church of which she had been a consistent member, James Lyndon's wife was laid in her last resting place. The bereaved husband was consoled for the mysterious visitation of Providence by the long funeral train, the solemn splendor of the trappings, the pious and respectful sympathy accorded him by his brothers and sisters in the Lord.

The preacher delivered a beautiful sermon, full of consolation and approbation. "A loving husband," he said, "and nine young children had been bereft by the wise hand of God whose kind and hidden purpose none could clearly see. The ways of Providence were mysterious and it seemed strange that a mother should be called away from the family that so much needed her." The interchanged glance between Hagar and her mother's sister expressed plainly "Not strange at all," but no one else saw it. "But peace and consolation would come to the faithful," the minister went on; "the pious husband would be soothed by the word of the Lord; he might build his hopes on His promise that he would meet her in Heaven," etc., etc.

And so the examplary wife and mother who had never whispered a sorrow in human ears, was buried. The neighbors went home to gossip the rest of the day, as the holiday-like feeling that a respectable funeral always gives, made it impossible to go to work. The Lyndon family went back to their desolate home where no love or sympathy between father and children lightened the gloom. A maiden sister of Mr. Lyndon's had been sent for to come and keep house and was expected in a few days. Hagar stole away to see Lucy as soon as she could but Dan would not let even her remain near her long. In all the world Hagar saw nothing bright or pleasant to comfort her.

Lucy's fever finally spent itself. She had sunk into a deep, deep slumber that Dan had been watching all day; the red skies of sunset were throwing a lurid light over all things, the wind that had swept and shrieked about the little cot all day was falling away to a low moan and Dan himself was wearily drowsing in the arm chair by the bedside. Suddenly a weak voice broke the silence.

"Dan, did you kill Harter?"

He sprang to his feet. Surprise, anger, anxiety intermingled, prompted the movement. The voice sounded sane—had Lucy come to herself again? He knew it was a critical moment and that Lucy must be kept quiet but the savage in him was roused by the question—the first conscious words she had uttered.

"Why? would you break your heart over it if I had?"

"I don't want to stay with a man who has murdered another— that's all. I should get up, weak as I am and run away——" the faint voice broke even under the momentary excitement and the white eyelids closed. Dan quickly gave her a cordial and lifted her head on his arm.

"I am a brute, Lucy, to let you get excited at such a time. There, there don't worry. I had a scuffle with him and a pistol went off but nobody was hurt. I scared him so he left on the train and will never be seen in these parts again. Lucy, did you and that man ever——" then he recollected himself; this was too disturbing a subject to converse upon in Lucy's weak state. He laid her head on the pillow and took a few turns up and down the room until he could control himself.

"Did we ever do anything criminal you mean. No, Dan, I swear it."

"But you were going to run away with him?"

"Give me something to give me a little strength, Dan, then I'll talk to you." He administered a few drops of stimulant then stood looking at her gloomily. A long silence followed. Then she said in a much stronger tone but sadder, "Dan, I have no mother now, have I?"

He shook his head.

"And I am so alone, and so young, so unfit for the place I am in. You ought to pity me, Dan, not blame. Have you taken care of me all the time I've been sick?" He nodded.

"All alone? all yourself?"

"Yes, of course."

"You've done it tenderly too, Dan. I am grateful, very grateful. I ought to like you and be contented, but oh! Dan, *think*—I never had any girlhood—the burdens of womanhood settled on me so soon. You have frightened and worried me, both with your love and your angry fits. We have to live so poor; I can never dress as one of my age likes to; I never have any amusements or pleasures. I think I was hardly old enough to love my children as I ought to, and they have tied me down so much. It is no wonder that I listened to kind words, to praise and finally to promises of a brighter and happier life. I was so tired of all this. I suppose I would have gone, Dan, if the train had not been late and he had met me."

"Damn him!' exclaimed Dan clenching his fist, "I wish I *had* killed him." He stamped up and down the room a few times then succeeded in quieting himself.

"But I did not mean to be wicked. I meant to work for my living until—until you had got a divorce and then perhaps honestly marry him."

"To the devil with your 'meant to's.' Do you know where he'd have landed you? No, you little ignoramus, you don't. Now remember you never *can* get away from me—I'll keep you a virtuous woman in spite of yourself. You'll stay with me and obey me, work for me, take care of my children. If you had stood before me a well woman and told me what you 'meant' to do, I should have given you a good thrashing likely, but I'd have kept you just the same."

Lucy began to cry.

"All my life before me! And no mother to comfort me! Oh mother, mother! Why did you die and leave me?" Her weakened frame shook with her sobs and her eyes looked wild. Dan saw this would not do; and with one of his quick changes of mood he knelt at her side, took her head on his shoulder, softly smoothed her brow and brushed away her tears.

"There, there, Lucy, don't cry. You know I love you. I love you so much I can't bear to have another man look at you, and you must be all mine while we both live. There, there, don't cry and make yourself sick again."

And so, gradually, she grew quiet and dropped into slumber. This was their reconciliation; in this fitful, fierce, savage sort of love, the ignorant, undisciplined boy and girl must find what happiness they could, for their bonds were life long.

IX

Children, Obey Your Parents

Another year. The brown cottage was clean and shining as a
new pin. Not a book, paper, toy, or old garment strewed the
spotless floor, not a speck of dust, not a childish finger-mark
soiled window-pane or furniture. If you came into the house at a
certain time of day, you saw six little smileless forms sitting in a
row, with books before their faces or some kind of work in their
hands, and on the wall behind them a bracket, across which three
or four switches lay. Or at certain other times of day, you saw
six little listless figures moving about a prescribed place in the
yard endeavoring to obey the order to "play," or again you found
each at some household duty, working mechanically without

words or laugher. Six I said, for the oldest boy had escaped, like a caged animal when a door is inadvertently left open, at the first opportunity, and Hagar had her own duties as systematically laid out. Every violation of Nature's creed: to be happy and free, was committed by those six little sinners every day of their lives, yet the neighbors all said,

"What a great improvement Miss Lyndon has made in that family, to be sure. The house is as orderly as a beehive, and the children are the quietest in the neighborhood. So orderly and obedient! She is a wonderful manager—most wonderful indeed!"

Hagar's heart ached for the little cribbed and disciplined brothers and sisters though her own numerous cares and worries were lessened by the severe system. No boisterous boys ran over and tormented her, there were no quarrels to settle, no shielding to be done. Exact justice was meted out to each one, and Hagar had little to do with the poor things but to answer pitiful looks from the appealing eyes, with glances full of love and encouragement.

Hagar was growing really beautiful. Her form was filling out and presented delicate, graceful curves, her face rounded, while a soft pink flush tinted the cheeks, already cleared of their old sallowness. Her great, dark eyes, always deep and wonderful, were grown luminous and soft, and brightened her expression as the gentle radiance of the stars lend loveliness to a beautiful

night. She was thoughtful and serious, not given to much
talking, and so imbued with a sort of sweet patience blended
with certain firmness and dignity that every one loved her while
they instinctively deferred to her. Her one confidential friend
was her journal kept in an old account book and hidden beneath
the boards of her little bed room. And the books she read were
never openly displayed; for the Bible, Pilgrim's Progress and
Heavenward Thoughts had long since ceased to satisfy her, and
the Lyndon system had no department under which fiction or
liberal literature could be admitted. Paul Deane often joined
her in her walks and errands, always accompanied her to church
and now and then came in and sat the evening out. But the cold
restraint of the household chilled them both—they could never
be frank and friendly in their conversations there as elsewhere.
As parties and picnics were forbidden pleasures, Hagar had little
opportunity to cultivate society or make new friends; the girls
who were her neighbors were not at all to her taste, and even
Lucy, though she felt a tender, pitying affection for her, could not
respond to her many undefined aspirations. She had clandestinely
met Clive Daley once or twice and found she understood and
sympathized with her more closely than any one else—but, Paul
was her faithful friend, confidant and adviser after all.

But Hagar was growing in her heart quite rebellious.
The severe restrictions placed upon her thoughts and actions,

her work, her reading, her every occupation were becoming exceedingly irksome. Thanks to her aunt who had kept her at home and given her lessons herself, she was a good seamstress and much farther advanced in school studies than most girls of her age; she felt confident that she could earn her own living, relieve her father of the burden of her expenses as well as the embarrassment of her presence, for he never seemed at ease with her, for all his severity. She only waited a convenient time to announce her intentions.

Her sister Lucy in the mean time was no happier than before her escapade and forced reconciliation; she was never so well and strong as then, she was more peevish and discontented, and alternating between subservience and fear of Dan and defiance and scorn of him; their life was a series of quarrels, reconciliations, and wearied calms. An older woman with a firm, gentle character might have made a passably good man of Dan. A strong, forbearing nature might have brought Lucy nearer to a sweet, quiet womanhood. But bound as they were, with their undisciplined, unwise, passionate natures, the result could but be continuous turbulence.

One morning Miss Lyndon found two radical books under Hagar's pillow. With stern, imposing visage she brought them down between thumb and finger with her apron intervening, and laid them before Mr. Lyndon.

"Eh! Where did such stuff as this come from? Hagar!"

"I sent the money for one and borrowed the other," answered Hagar, trying bravely to overcome the old, childish fear of her father's authority.

"Do you dare to read such vile trash in defiance of me?"

"It is not vile trash, father. I have learned more of truth and real goodness in those books than I ever thought of before. I am old enough and I know enough, father, to judge of the books I read, myself. I am an individual, as much as you are and you cannot think for me any more than I can for you."

Hagar was trembling with her unusual daring, but she looked very determined. Her father gazed at her in astonishment, and seemed to be deciding on what terrible penalty he should inflict; but the very enormity of the offense rendered anything he could do inadequate, and he said sternly:

"No woman ever becomes able to judge of the books she should read. *Never* look inside of such a book again. *I* will choose your reading for you, as I always have," and he lifted the stovelid and threw the volumes on the coals. Hagar sprang to save the borrowed one but it was too late—the edges were already curling up and blazing.

"I must have the money, father, to pay for that book. It isn't mine."

"My money shall never be used to pay Satan for his mischief."

"I must work for it then."

"I shall superintend the spending of any money you may earn—you are not of age yet."

"Not of age? What does that term mean? Up to a certain moment you have a right to tyrannize over me—even beat me as you please—the next, I am recognized as a woman with rights and responsibilities of my own. I don't believe in blind obedience of children at any time, and surely when I come to have thoughts, inclinations, aspirations and powers, apart from you I have a natural right to think, act and speak for myself. I do not think I *owe* you obedience, father."

"You are tainted with the abominable stuff you've been reading. I will not hear another word out of your head. I won't argue with my own child. Only remember this—at the first act of disobedience on your part you leave my house forever."

Nothing more was said at that time, but Hagar's mind was more fully made up than ever, to seek independence and freedom. She had odd ideas about freedom and responsibility for so young a girl, but whatever they were she was true to herself.

Soon after Miss Daley made one of her visits to the town. It is hard to say why the lady came back so often to the spot where every one knew her but to point the finger of scorn at her; but a bitter defiance was part of her nature, and, if we can allow that such a woman may be endowed with some tenderness, perhaps an interest in her sister's children and in her sister's grave.

Hagar met her driving through the street, and she came to a sudden decision. She asked her aunt to take her in and drive out through the country lanes.

"If you realize what you are doing, Hagar, and have counted the cost—all right—but you should think well of it."

"I want to talk to you and if you do not object I will not ask any one else."

"All right, come on then.

"Now what is it, little one? I knew you had some new purpose in your dear solemn face as soon as I saw you."

"First, I want a true friend. I want to know if I am right, or if I am unnaturally wicked. I have always been so curbed and checked and disciplined, I cannot always see what is best. Other people make me feel bitter, rebellious and impatient. You never do—why is it?"

"Poor little girl. I wish you had a better, wiser friend than your reckless and unfortunate aunt. The greatest kindness I can do you is keep away from you."

"I have never seen anything but good in you. And any way, I have a life of my own to live. I must be myself—I am so hampered and restrained where I am, I am miserable." Hagar went on to tell of her determination and asked her aunt's advice and sympathy. No one could be better fitted to warn the young of dangers than one who knew all about them, and Clive's advice was sound and wholesome when she saw that argument would not keep Hagar in the old home much longer. Secretly she resolved to never come near her in her future position wherever it might be, though Hagar counted much on her companionship. They met many people who knew them and great were the stares of astonishment; in a very few minutes it was quite generally known that Hagar was out riding with her disreputable aunt. Even Paul saw them and bowed with sad and serious surprise. Hagar looked troubled for a moment but thought she could soon make it all right with him when they met, and cleared her face with the cheery determination she had decided upon.

When their ride was ended and Hagar arrived at her own gate, Mr. Lyndon was waiting for her, with a shocked, forbidding countenance.

"You have disobeyed me and disgraced yourself and your family, you wicked girl!"

"I am willing to take the natural consequences of my own actions," Hagar tried to answer quietly.

"One of them is that you leave my house for ever. Pack your clothes and take enough money to keep you off the streets for a month—you will sink there quick enough—and go."

"Very well, father."

She entered the house, gathered up her few belongings, and went out of it, carrying her satchel, a stranger to it forever more. She would go to Lucy's for one night and in the morning go to a distant city and find a place where an old schoolmate, in a large dressmaking establishment worked. She would come back in the morning and say good by to the children and aunt Lyndon—her father she would probably never see again. She looked after him as he put on his hat and walked away, wondering if any feeling of tenderness or regret lingered in his bosom, but apparently there was none, for he never looked back.

Lucy was astonished, angered and dismayed, and scolded at her sister with vehemence if not with judgment. But she loved her after all and shed tears on her neck when she bade her good bye in the morning. "You might have married and had a home of your own, Hagar. Now what is to become of you?"

"I shall get a home of my own in time without marrying."

She said a last good bye finally, and went back to her old home, bade her aunt a cold farewell, kissed the tearful children all around, and went out from her father's house, a poor, friendless girl, ignorant of the world, but free.

Across the fence the neighbor women gossiped:

"That Hagar Lyndon is going to the bad—isn't it awful?"

"You don't say! And she was so carefully raised, too. Why there ain't a stricter man in town than Mr. Lyndon, and Mrs. Lyndon, poor soul, though she was kind o' incapable, was *so* respectable and quiet, and her aunt Lyndon is one of the best managers of a family you ever saw. I am awfully astonished. But what's she done?"

"Why she's gaddin' about with that Clive Daley all the time and every body knows what *she* is. Goes out ridin' with her, and I guess even stays at her room in the hotel. Any way, she's been going on so bad that her father has turned her out of his house."

"For the land's sake! Why, I'm kind o' sorry for the poor girl. Where'll she go?"

"I heard she was going to W——, a pretty good-sized town, to work at dressmaking. Laws a mercy! I'm afraid she won't work at anything so respectable, very long."

"Why, there she goes down the street with Paul Deane. Is she going away on the train this forenoon, did you say? She's going the wrong way if she is—but it's most an hour yet. Now Deane is a real nice young man and he wouldn't be seen with her if he thought she was very bad."

"Oh she's got him bewitched long ago. He'd think everything she did was just right, no matter what it was."

"Why that's a pity. For he is such a goodlooking young fellow, smart and industrious and a good printer. Why he could take full charge of the newspaper today if he wanted to. They do say though, he's inclined to be something of an infidel,—if it wasn't for that he could marry any young lady in town."

"Well, maybe—though I guess my Maria could have had him go with her if she'd given him any encouragement—but of course she thinks highly of him. I must go and look after my bread"—for between a wish to impress upon her friend, the captivating powers of her daughter and the fear that what she said would be repeated to the young man, she felt she was getting into difficulties and so hurried away.

X

Love's Young Dream

What were Paul and Hagar saying as they walked together for the last time down her native village street?

Paul was troubled evidently, for his grey eyes were very serious and his white brow was knitted with an unusual scowl.

"But I do not see as it is necessary to defy public opinion, your father's command and my—your friend's wishes in such an open manner. Remember I do not believe you have merited being turned out of your home, but you have been indiscreet."

"Yes, I know you think so, Paul, and I would not displease you willingly, but I know only good of Aunt Clive. I have long determined to go away and earn my own living and this is only an opportunity, I want to belong to myself. I wish to choose my own friends, select my own reading, act for myself, and think my own thoughts. I am willing to work hard, if part of the time I may be entirely my own mistress."

"You do not know the world, Hagar. You do not know how very hard it will be to struggle for existence alone. And with your unconventional, independent ways of thinking, society will misunderstand you, and sting you, and hinder you on every side."

"I feel strong enough to overcome all difficulties; and you need not fear for my own conduct while I have so severe a critic to please—my own self respect."

"But I cannot bear to see you go away alone. Stay here— please do not interrupt me, for I have something very near to my heart to say to you."

They were out of the village now, where the grassy borders of the street, the shade of trees, and the stillness, made it like a country lane.

"You must know, Hagar, how dear you are to me. We have grown up together; I can scarcely remember a time when I did not come to you for sympathy and advice in all my troubles. It will not be living when I never see you more. Stay here, Hagar, and marry me. I am poor but I know we wouldn't mind that for a few years. You are silent. Have you no affection for me?"

"Yes, so much that I cannot bear to give you pain. We have been very happy as friends, Paul. I hope we may yet be happy in our friendship. But I cannot marry you. I never shall marry any one."

"Oh, you cannot mean that! I have heard that all girls say the same while they are young but they change their minds sooner or later, if indeed they ever meant it."

"I do not say this from any girlish whim. I value your esteem and peace of mind too much to trifle, if it were not of itself a serious subject to me. I have carried it deep in my soul—I have had it imprinted on my heart with suffering. I resolved long ago never to be a wife. Young, strong, glowing with health and spirits as we are now, it seems a beautiful thing to give ourselves to each other. We would be happy, deliriously happy for a time, and then, we would wake up, to misery."

"What, you and I? We would always be happy. With you beside me, I would defy fate, sorrow, poverty, everything."

"Other lovers have talked so—thousands of them. And yet look around and see if you can call to mind one married couple wedded five years who look, act and appear as you hope and expect we will appear after five years married life. You cannot think of one. They are old while yet young; they grow faded and worn; they harass and irritate each other—they are sickly and unhappy. This, when both are ordinarily well-behaved people.

When men choose to be tyrannical, the case becomes much more pitiable—more deplorable.

"Do you imagine I could ever misuse you?"

"No, it is not in you *knowingly* to wrong a single living thing. But we would wrong each other. We would no longer be two individuals, with two free, independent characters. We would drag on each other. And, to the best man living, the wife is more or less, a slave: the nature of the marriage institution, custom, the church, the inherent tendencies of men themselves through ages of rulership, all go to make her so. I would never be a comfortable slave, to myself or my owner."

"As if I would ever make you that. Surely, knowing the rocks ahead we can steer clear of them. You shall always be your own mistress, Hagar."

"You think you can, in one moment of time give me myself, through years of future bondage. *You* may not be the same ten years from now. Power spoils the best of men. You are noble and generous, but I would ever be at the mercy of a change in you; and you would be a wonderful man indeed, if, in the face of custom, through hard work, poverty and struggle with that power always at your hand, you should never seek to use it.

"I have wept and groaned in hidden anguish even as a child, over the sorrows of poor men's wives. Do you know, Paul, I have never shed a tear over my mother's death? It is not that

I am hard hearted—it is because I loved her. My mother was a slave. No black woman of the south was ever a more complete one. She bore ten children and I cannot remember when her face was calm and free from lines of pain, until I saw it, sweet and peaceful in death. I have known delicate women beaten by big, rough men for rebelling in their slavery; and all around us in this very town are sad, sickly-looking women with more children about their knees than they know what to do with, slowly dying as respectable, virtuous, obedient wives, when all they need is *freedom* and *rest*. It may seem strange to hear a young girl talk like this, but I have grown old with others' suffering."

"But I, dear Hagar, would only protect you; you cannot always live alone. Give me the right to be near you, to work for you, and love you, and I swear that you shall always be as free as you are today."

"You think so, Paul," and she gave his ardent, earnest face a fond, proud look through a mist of tears. "You make it hard for me to be firm. But you cannot pledge your whole future away thus. There is not time to say more now; I must hasten back and I would rather say good by to you here. Sometimes I will write to you and I shall expect good long answers, frank and friendly and like yourself, in return."

"But may I come and see you sometime? You haven't told me anything of your plans. Have you anything definite in view? And tell me—have you money—money enough?"

"Oh yes, my father gave me some and Aunt Daley sent me quite a sum in a way that I could not refuse it without wronging her. I am to enter a dressmaking establishment as an apprentice where a schoolmate is working. I shall be safe and in a good place—do not fear for me. I cannot say, come and visit me, but— wait until I send for you."

"Don't be too cruelly long about it then."

"And one word more, Paul. Don't let my decision make your life unhappy. If you ever meet any one with whom you think you can be happy, and she loves you, marry. We can still be friends. I will kiss you once, Paul, for a good bye—it will be for a long, long time."

She gave him her hand and offered her lips; but he laid her young head on his breast and pressed her cheek with his hand; and when he had tenderly, reverently kissed her, turned away and left her, with no uttered words of good by.

XI

Faithful unto Death

Hagar in her new home soon fell into a regular routine that for many months was undisturbed by any unusual event. Quick with her hands, ready with taste and ingenuity, willing and industrious, her employer, Madame Anele, soon found it to her own interest to advance her to the best position in the establishment. She had found a quiet boarding place where several other working women lived cheaply but respectably, and shared her room with a woman no longer young, whose face told a story of trouble and care, but who talked little of herself, or, in fact of anything else. Hagar liked her rather the better for this, as she was inclined to study and thoughtfulness, and a gay, chattering room-mate would have become very irksome to her. She was of too quiet a nature to become a favorite of the girls with whom she came in contact, though there was not one but trusted her implicitly and would have been sure of her sympathy and assistance in case of trouble. But she liked being left to herself; and thus in days of not uncongenial work, and evenings of study with now and then a concert or lecture, her quiet life flowed on.

It is unusual for the young, with health, active brains, and warm hearts to be satisfied with so monotonous an existence. But to Hagar, freedom from actual trouble, the absence of constant restraint, the opportunity to read what she liked, to hear progressive thoughts dropped from noble lips, to go and come, to think, act and speak without continual criticism—were delights enough for her who had lived always under a weight of these troubles. She received letters from Lucy occasionally and, as often as she would answer, long interesting ones from Paul. Her sister's scrawls were full of petty trifles, gossip, complaints and scoldings about Dan; only that they linked her to her old home when mother was in it, and the brothers and sisters she pitied so much, she would rather not receive them. Paul's were very different. His mind, like hers, was developing, and in each dwelt an aspiration for truth wherever found, that their correspondence quickened and inspired. No subject was too profound, or too sacred for discussion; and thus, though separated in body, in thought they advanced together. All references to love as between themselves beyond expressions of remembrance and esteem, Hagar persistently set aside.

The time went on until three silent but busy years went by, which left their impress on Hagar in the added beauty of face and form, in the growth of mind and character and in the fixing of certain principles in her determined spirit.

One evening Esther Copeland, her room-mate, sat down, work in hand with an air of having something unusual to say. Between these two, a quiet but deep friendship had grown up. They were of that unusual class of women who *can* live together for years and not find fault with each other. Each accorded the other perfect liberty, neither ever intruded with curious questions, reproaches, criticisms or unasked advice. Each respected the other's individual rights, and whether silent or conversing they understood one another, and a fine, unexpressed sympathy smoothed over every little jar that might have disturbed their harmonious companionship.

"What is it Esther?" asked Hagar laying down her book on the lamp stand between them. "I know you have something to tell me."

"Why yes—or that is—I don't know whether it will interest you or not. But, for several days I have noticed an old man, or one who is weak and trembling, maybe from sickness or drink rather than from age, loitering about our street, appearing to keep an eye on this building. Tonight he spoke to me as I was coming up the steps. He says:

"Miss Hagar Lyndon lives here, doesn't she?" I answered that she did; then he muttered something that sounded like "I s'pose she wouldn't know anything about me."

"Do you want to see her?" I asked.

"Well no," he said hesitating, "I've no particular business with her and she wouldn't care to see me. I used to know her family, that's all."

"Miss Lyndon would see you if you ask for her I expect," I told him, and he shuffled away saying something about "not troubling you." I turned to ask his name just as I had my hand on the door knob but he had got out of hearing."

"I wonder who it can be?" queried Hagar. "Certainly I would see him if it is some one who used to know us. Perhaps he wanted to ask for help. Was he poor? Was he a rough sort of person?"

"He looked poor enough and considerably run down, but as though he might have been a tolerable well-looking man sometime."

"If you see him again, Esther, bring him into the hall—I suppose our land-lady would object to our bringing him into the sitting room—and let me know. At least it will do no harm to talk to him."

Two or three days passed in which nothing more was heard or seen of the strange man. Then it happened that Hagar came home before Esther. A shivering figure leaned against a pillar of the porch and slowly reached out his hand.

"Are you Hagar Lyndon?"

"Yes. What do you want of me? Do I know you?"

"I want—I am in want of everything. I never thought I'd come to beg, but I've eaten nothing for two days and I am sick and tired out. If you knew all about me you wouldn't stop to pity or speak to me, I suppose. I know your folks. I've had you in my arms when you were a mite of a girl. I've been a bad man— you'd curse me if you knew—but I can't help now—pride all gone—help a poor fellow with a small loan"—the man's haggard face suddenly turned whiter, he tottered and fell at her feet. He moaned as he lay and murmured a name brokenly, "Clive Daley."

"Oh, what shall I do with him?" Hagar exclaimed more troubled and perplexed than she had been for a long time. I am afraid he is dying. He spoke my Aunt's name—perhaps he was some dear friend of hers, and I have no place to take him. Oh! there comes Esther. Look, Esther, is this the man who spoke to you? He began to talk to me and then fell at my feet. Is he dying?"

Esther seldom moved out of her usual calm, serious demeanor, bent quietly down and looked at the man.

"It is the same person and he is not dying but in a faint. I will call a policeman."

After some time one was found who came and roughly turned him over. "Oh, yes; it's Tom Lowell. He's been totterin' about here for days;—had some notion of runnin' him in on general principles; but he's got sort of a claim on a kind of a room down here on Bailey Street—we'll take him there."

Hospital ambulances and patrol wagons were not as handy at this time in the smaller cities as now and it took considerable time and red tape to convey a sufferer to a hospital and have him admitted. The officer merely called another one, and between them they half carried, half dragged the insensible man along the pavement.

"Let us go with them, Esther. I want to learn more about him and see what kind of a condition they will leave him in."

"I'm ready. He's a needy human being whatever else he's been in his life."

"Tom Lowell, the police called him. I don't know that I ever heard the name before, but I want to learn more about him."

They followed through many streets and around many corners until they stopped in the most miserable portion of the city. The man was taken up a dilapidated stairway in a tumble down house, through a dirty, narrow hall and into a small, miserable room containing a wretched bed, a broken chair and an old drygoods box; here the officers left him, considering their duty done. But the two women could not leave any one thus. They sent for a doctor, and did what they could for the sick man's comfort.

"He's simply drank and starved himself to death," was the indifferent physician's verdict. "His days are numbered—can't do much for him. If he has any friends, better send for them. I have heard that he is of a good family, that they live somewhere in the east—they might be willing to bury him. Know them?"

"We do not; but he seems to know my aunt. She might know something about them."

"Better ask her. I'll call in the morning. Goodnight." And the blunt old doctor hurried away.

They looked at the wreck, lying so helpless and desolate in the bare, cold room. What could they do? No doubt he deserved his misery, and anyway he was a stranger to them; they were women and poor. Yet it seemed heartless to leave him alone in that poor place. He became conscious of their presence, presently, and began to talk brokenly.

"Tell Clive—please send for Clive—for Clive Daley. She'll come. She loved me once and she's not one to hold spite. It is a long time since I left her but I never could forget her, and now

I know my last days have come. I'd like to see her. Will you please—send and ask her to come and see me just once?"

Hagar promised. They asked some people in another room if they would not look in on the sick man once in a while and give him the medicine left by the doctor, they rather sulkily agreed to do so. Then they went out into the now darkened streets, and hurried home. But on their way they stopped and telegraphed to Clive the little they knew about the man and that he had asked for her.

That evening after supper the two sat on either side of their little table as usual, Hagar with her books, Esther with her endless sewing; but Hagar was not reading. Her hands were clasped behind her head and she was thinking.

"Do you know, we've done a very shocking thing today Esther," she said presently. "We—two lone, single women have followed to his wretched home a dissipated worn out vagabond, who has been I suppose at some time a follower of that disreputable woman—than whom a better one never lived—my aunt. There we waited on him when no one else would. I wonder why?"

"Because we would have been unhappy to stay snugly and respectably at home not knowing what had become of that poor man. But goodness! Miss Hagar, such things are not so new to me. Maybe if you knew how much of downright trouble I've been through—trouble that takes one right down into misery, poverty, coarseness—not the kind you can set down in a comfortable room and brood over sentimentally—you wouldn't care about being a friend and companion to me."

"Why Esther! I hope you know me too well to think that. I've been familiar with sordid, wearing, unromantic troubles all my life and I would but love you the more to know what you have suffered. I can read much more in your face than you have ever told me but if you were to relate your story to me it might bring us nearer each other and benefit us both."

"My story will not sound like those in books and it isn't interesting at all; but if you care to hear it, it may relieve me to tell it. I never told people around here whether I was married or not, but I guess they call me an old maid. Well, I *was* married when only sixteen—ran away from an unpleasant home to do so. I thought I was very much in love, and the man I married was one that would be obeyed. I never gave much thought to money but s'posed he would of course provide for me. In a very little while, I found he was tyrannical, penniless and opposed to working himself. He drank a great deal—not in saloons or with crowds, but in a sulky, solitary way in his home. In fact he never was away from home and that is why my life got to be so very hard to bear. I was his slave. We lived in two poor little rooms and I had to bring home cheap sewing to do, because he would not let me stay away all day to work. I earned our living by hard toil but that I could have borne, for I was strong, if only I could have done it in peace. There are somethings it is hard to tell a young unmarried woman, things that seldom *are* told, but that cause more misery, insanity, sickness, even death than any other one cause. Night and day I had to be at his beck and call, until life held only an awful disgust for me. Nobody ever saw him reel the streets drunk, or haunt saloons or disreputable places, he never stayed away nights and people wondered, except that we were poor, why I looked so haggard and unhappy. But what to other people seemed to be his virtues was my curse. He *was* dissipated, drunken, licentious, bad—but it was all within the four walls of his home. I was the sole companion and victim of his orgies. Sometimes I was not allowed to sleep until near morning; then I had to work as hard as ever the next day, or we would starve. At last I began to resist and say I would not stand such a life. Then he beat me and one night when he was sound asleep I got up and ran away. I walked to another city and found work in a kitchen. He traced me there, finally, and made so much trouble the family made me go away with him because he was my husband, and they could not be bothered with him. I tried life again with him only to find it worse than before. Time after time I ran away from him only to have him find me and demand me as his wife, so that the people with whom I worked would send me away with him for the sake of peace. At last he died; the strongest constitution could not endure the drains he made upon it, and when I was twenty three I was free, but looking as old and careworn as I do today. I've worked hard in different places since then, but I've been at peace and I do not mind it. I have had a horror of men as husbands ever since; of course there are good men and I respect them, but it gives the best of them too much power—the customs and laws, I mean, and every body thinks their rights must be respected above everything else."

Hagar clasped the woman's hand in sympathy as she ceased speaking. "You are right. There is a new bond between us now."

XII

He That Is Without Sin
Let Him Cast the First Stone

Hagar remained at home the next morning to receive Clive Daley if she came. About noon she arrived, looking, Hagar thought, more disturbed than she had ever seen her.

"Tell me," she asked almost with her first greeting, "Is it Lowell?"

"The policeman called him Tom Lowell."

Clive sank into a seat trembling. "It's Tom," she murmured, "after all these years. It's the man I loved, Hagar—my poor baby's father."

"Is it possible? Then you will not go near him, will you? He was a bad, cruel man to desert you at such a time."

"Oh, I must go to him. He needs help; he is poor—maybe dying. I know he was weak and cowardly in that old time, but he has had trouble enough no doubt. You know, Hagar, he ran away from home when he was a boy, without a cent, and he had never been raised to work. He met me and we loved each other, but dared not marry because we were so poor. I think Tom believed if he were out of the way my sister's husband would do something for me. He! I might have looked for help to some degraded old thief, but not to him with all *his* piety and virtue. I *have* felt bitter towards Tom all these years, but not as I have toward those who drove me to despair and let my baby die. I know the man I hate is your father but——"

"The deed was none the less cruel, aunt, and I have always felt it deeply."

"Well—now that Tom needs me and is poor and sick I shall go and see him."

Hagar prepared a hasty lunch and very soon after they started for Lowell's miserable place. She did not go in with her aunt, feeling that the first meeting between the two would better be unwitnessed. Asking her to come back in the evening she left her, and went on to her work for the afternoon.

Clive came in late in the evening. Hagar had never seen her face look so softened and tender, her manners so quiet and gentle.

"Think how much I have done today, Hagar. I found Tom—poor fellow—how he wept when he saw me! He is a wreck of his old self but I cannot forget that I loved him once. I found him, I began to say, in such a wretched place I could not bear to see him there another hour. I went and rented rooms in a good, quiet hotel and had him removed. I had him given a warm bath, then some nourishing food that he could bear, and made him comfortable. You should have seen how grateful he was. Then he cried and begged me if I did not think him sunk too low to—to marry him and stay with him. If I did not know, Hagar, that he can never get well I should not have considered it for a moment. But—I could not care for him as I wish, and I could not desert him—and so, dear girl—I have just married him."

Hagar looked grave.

"I suppose I ought to congratulate you, aunt."

"No you need not. It would not do for us to marry were he to live. I've taken the only means that gives me a right to remain by a dying man's bedside. I told him what I have been—it seemed to shock him at first, then he said,

"I, as a man have done worse, and I deserted you, Clive."

She soon went away.

The sick man lingered several weeks. No woman could have been more untiring, more devoted than Clive. It was her care that kept him living as long as he did; indeed he owed every comfort he had to her.

One day he said he wanted to make a will. Clive thought it a sick man's whim, for what had he to leave? and tried to evade his request. But he insisted so strongly that to please him she called in a lawyer to write the will, and dispose of it in the proper way.

"I seem a poor enough wretch here today," he said, "with my wife paying for every mouthful I eat. But if I haven't any money I ought to have, and I want you to fix up the will so that everything I may have a legal title to at this moment shall go to Clive when I am gone. I have been a hard customer and I've never written to my friends back east, but I've an idea they haven't all forgotten me. For myself I never should have hunted up the matter, but for her sake who has done so much for me, I want what is my own. And when the will is made out and signed I'll tell you where to look up my folks and you see if there isn't a little inheritance coming to me."

Now the lawyer took a decided interest in the business, and Clive looked on with a startled surprise. The paper was duly made out and signed and the lawyer went away to attend to his later request.

In a little over a week he came in with an air of pleased and business-like importance. Tom Lowell had grown very weak, and was lying propped up with pillows so that he could look out upon the evening sky, holding Clive's hand in his own. It was evident that his hours were numbered.

"Can you bear good news?" said the lawyer cautiously.

"Yes, indeed. Did you find I was right?"

"You were. There is a little matter of ten thousand dollars, been waiting for you over a year. Nobody knew where you were and the other heirs were trying to prove you dead so as to divide the sum. I wrote just in time. It can be placed in your hands in less than a week's time."

"In Clive's, you mean." A happy smile broke over his worn, haggard face that made it almost handsome.

"Ah dear, I can make up in some degree for what you have suffered, and for all your kindness to me. And you need never go back to that horrible life again."

He laid his cheek against her hand and seemed to sink into slumber; but he never spoke again and before morning he had passed away.

And so Clive found herself left alone again, but with a competence. A change came over her after Lowell's death. She seemed quiet and peaceful, but sad. All her old boldness and bitterness were gone; much of her strength and vivacity left her

too, for she seemed strangely weak, and slow in her movements.
She established herself in a comfortable house in the city
and none knowing her history she was looked upon as a very
deserving and respectable widow to whom it was worth while to
be polite. But Clive kept very much to her self; she did not wish
to receive attentions she knew would not be given if her story
was known, and she cared little for society in general, at best. Her
charities were many; and so, for some time she pursued a peaceful
kindly life, that brought happiness to many.

She and Hagar might have been brought to make their
home together but for a natural reserve on both sides. Hagar
feared that she might be suspected of wishing to profit by her
aunt's money. Clive did not think best to offer to join her
broken life with that of a young, innocent girl. Her purse she
declared was ever at Hagar's disposal; indeed Hagar need not have
worked at all but that she refused to accept her aunt's generosity.
Independence and liberty were as yet dearer to her than aught
else. Her daily work was not uncongenial. Having mastered the
details of her trade and being naturally industrious and in every
way reliable, Madame Anele, the lady for whom she worked, had
great confidence in her and already placed many responsibilities
in her charge; this relieved her from the irksomeness of daily
toil to some extent. She was well liked by the girls in the workroom but she had no intimate friends among them. Original,

thoughtful, independent women seldom find intimates among their own class—there is so little that is congenial between them. The lady of the establishment herself, came the nearest to being a confidential friend, for she seemed to like Hagar and look to her for advice and encouragement more than to any one else.

XIII

Chains of Crystal and
Bonds of Cobweb

Madame Anele was a very fashionable, very proper personage, with great business ability and wonderful capacities for pleasing. Her business was prosperous and she owned the home in which she lived. Her family consisted of two beautiful children, and a husband who was as much as possible kept out of the sight of the public, being neither useful nor ornamental in any capacity. She liked to speak of her husband in a dignified, respectable way, as befitting a popular and exemplary member of church and a certain model circle; but the less seen of him the better. He seldom frequented the house except when he wanted money. The only variation in his appearance was from slightly intoxicated, through the intermediate stages to a drunken stupor and he was ugly and disagreeable in all of them. One evening Hagar remained late to look over some accounts and assist Madame Anele in making out some bills. They left the big, empty workroom and entered the little cosy back parlor where Madame spent most of her leisure time. After some time spent in business Madame Anele pushed back the books and said,

"I wonder that you do not marry, Miss Lyndon. One so fitted to adorn any society, so collected, so easy—so well adapted to rich surroundings—how is it you prefer to toil?"

Madame Anele was not as French as her name as written on her cards would indicate, but she assumed a certain broken style of speech for effect. Hagar smiled:

"Am I not well enough situated? Besides, if I cared to change, who is there to give me 'rich surroundings' and place me where I may 'adorn society'?"

"Ah! now you talk, Miss Lyndon. I know the very one—a relative—rich, handsome, amiable. He was here one day—you passed through the show-room—he looked, admired, was enthused. He would know you at once, but I put him off—I would prepare the way. I will describe him—you cannot but be pleased, and then I will plan a meeting. Ah! I am in my element now."

"I am sorry to disappoint you, Madame, but it is useless to take so much trouble for me. I am very well satisfied as I am."

"Of course—that is perfectly proper. *I* will arrange everything."

At this moment, as Hagar was turning away with a faint expression of disgust upon her face, Madame's objectionable husband came in. He was more than usually intoxicated, more than usually disagreeable. He wanted money, he wanted his wife to be more dutiful, he found fault more than was customary. Hagar had seen him several times before but had never been a witness of quite so repugnant a scene as this; for his wife scolded and berated him and finally got rid of him by giving all the money she had in the house, making him promise to keep himself out of sight for at least a week.

Hagar would have gone away but that she felt Madame Anele preferred she should stay.

"Why do you not rid yourself of that man altogether?" Hagar asked seeing that a confidence in a way had been forced upon her.

"What is it you can mean? Rid myself of him! Kill him, do you think?"

"Heavens, no! Leave him, send him away, do not recognize him as your husband?"

"How is that possible? We are legally married: he belongs to me, I, to him. I cannot send him away."

"Why, do you love him? Does his presence ever give you pleasure?"

"No, no, I would be glad never to see him again."

"Then you wrong yourself to live with him a day."

"Would you advise me to *separate*—to *divorce* myself? Ah! that would be too terrible! A divorcee! I could never endure to be that."

"Can you endure this life easier? You are independent—you earn all the means for providing for your family; he is simply a burden and a sorrow to you. You would be happier, freer, to send him away."

"Ah! to picture life without him—that is too much! But it is impossible. I could not bear the disgrace. Our church forbids divorce except for one cause, and that is in a man often excusable; besides he would not go away and let me alone. He knows the law gives him a right to stay with his family."

"But in reality he has *no* right. He does nothing for you, he keeps you in misery, your children in fear, and a constant danger before you of bringing more children into existence under such terrible conditions. He is a pensioner on your bounty with a permit from the church to be your master."

"Miss Lyndon, Miss Lyndon—you say fearful things. You know one marries for better or for worse and one may not throw aside such sacred ties for a little trouble. What God hath joined together let no man put asunder."

"Do you believe God had anything to do with joining you two when scenes like tonight are of constant recurrence?"

Madame Anele gave a deep sigh but shook her head.

"I could not break my marriage vows or I could no longer pray; then I would be desolate. And then the disgrace! No, no, I cannot leave my husband."

Hagar had taken the lovely girl who had come into the room on her lap and was curling her soft golden hair over her fingers; the baby boy lay on the sofa asleep. Her heart hungered over these children and many times a day, when they were near, she bent and kissed or fondled them. She pressed the child closely to her now as she said,

"Oh well, you are incorrigible in your misery. You have your darling children to comfort you, and after all——," she gazed with a yearning dreaminess in her eyes at the pretty child.

"Ah! you see, Miss Lyndon. You will yourself yield and take up the yoke with the rest of us, for you are a natural mother. You will not live without the little ones to bless."

Hagar arose, placed the child in the mother's arms and prepared to go. At the door she looked back at the bright home picture. The tasteful, well-lighted parlor, the beautiful boy asleep on the couch, the pretty mother lovingly clasping her little girl in her arms. A deep sigh escaped her. Somehow the vision of what she had shut her heart against, struck her with painful force tonight. She had never realized all that her resolution implied. A long, dreary life of childlessness!

But she only said "good night" and went out into the darkness.

"That, or a fearful price," she thought as she slowly walked toward her home. To live as so many women lived or remain childless! The one she had just left for instance. Not always does financial independence free the wife. She was the bread winner, yet she endured what any slave might. The chains of custom, religion and law held her tight, though economic necessity had no part in her bondage. Were her children sufficient consolation? Involuntarily Hagar shook her head.

Time glided on with occasional renewals of these scenes, but generally bringing only a quiet content to Hagar in her busy but uneventful life. Madame Anele had brought about an introduction to her favorite friend and was reveling in the delights and schemings of match-making. Hagar found Mr. Harold Hathaway an agreeable gentleman, with a seeming impulsiveness of manner that after all she guessed hid a still determined strength of will and character. He was intelligent and well informed enough to attract her attention and she did not dislike his companionship; but she laughed inwardly at Madame Anele's all too apparent maneuvers, and sighed when she thought how vain they were.

Lucy wrote that her father had married again. "You would not think," she scribbled, "what a difference there is in the 'old terror.' Aunt left the house the minute number 2 entered it for 'such trifling she couldn't stand' she said. Our mother-in-law is a fat, good looking, careless acting, good hearted woman who doesn't seem to care a snap for pa's scowls or growls, or to know that any such thing as order, system or rules exist for her. Actually, she laughs at the old man and he—would you believe it? seems to stand in awe of her. She has turned the children loose, lets them do as they please, won't have them whipped, and doesn't take a bit of care of them. They don't mind that, but don't they act and look like sin? Really the family is getting disreputable and the old man is helpless. She dresses up like a girl of sixteen, hires the heavy work done and don't mind pa no more'n if he wasn't around. Lord! I like her off hand style—wish I could gain it—wouldn't I make Dan toe the mark and never be miserable myself?"

Hagar felt sorry for her brothers and sisters—forced into a hard existence, curbed, repressed, punished through their earlier years, turned out, loveless, unguided, uncared for, with characters weakened by such a course—what could become of them? Any interference on her part would be resented by her father she well knew.

XIV

The Mother-Love

One evening, when the early Spring had borrowed a day from Summer to help her out with some belated buds she had in hand, Hagar wandered far, toward the edge of town instead of going directly home. The hour, the softness of the air rested soothingly upon her perturbed spirits, and lured her out into night's solitude. The dreams of girlhood, coming to her through strange, rough barriers were but troubled ones. What could she do with them and her resolutions together? The evening before the story of a man's love had been murmured in her ear; and today an unusual letter from Paul stirred her soul to its placid deaths. He swept aside with a man's strong impatient hand the petty barriers which

she had erected between herself and the expression of his love. He
wanted her. He knew that she was his own in heart and spirit and
he demanded the right to come and claim her. Hagar was startled
that his words thrilled her so; what was she to do with her life if it
was to be one struggle?

Then she thought of Harold Hathaway. He could give her a
position in society, comforts, luxuries, leisure, ease, opportunities
for study. She need not fear a waning of love, for their association
would begin with a calm friendship which time would but
strengthen; she need not fear a master for intuitively she felt
her own powers—springing from two sources—a superiority of
character, and the absence of a woman's love for him.

The years would peacefully come and go; children would
cluster around her knees; friends would bless her and life's
pathway be made smooth. And Paul? Would he remain her quiet,
wise, cool-headed friend? Could she ever look straight into his
eyes and claim his eternal respect? With a shudder she turned
away from that thought. Should she then in an abandonment of
love accept the happiness *he* offered her?

In the midst of a sweet, intoxicating dream, a vision of
her mother's white, worn face as she lay dead, with her baby on
her bosom, came to her. Then she saw her moving about their
plain home, slow, sad, submissive, suffering. Other memories
crowded up—Lucy's wrecked girlhood, the haggard, aged faces of

poor men's wives she had known in childhood, the cowed forms of women who had been beaten into submission, the narrow rancorous lives of loveless women seeking forgetfulness in fashion and excitement, the irritable, wearing, chafing companionship of those whose hot passions had consumed their love in early days of wedlock. The deep-seated bitterness and repugnance of her early girlhood returned with these memories, swept over her being with the rush of a returning tide and bore away all the creeping, dreamy tenderness which had hovered, almost daring to nestle within the recesses of her heart.

Marriage? Never, for her. Some time in the far off future woman might be strong enough, free enough, great enough to bend and love man to his own glory and hers—but not in her life-time; she might even have some little part toward bringing about that day, but not by yielding to the passing languor of a new stirring passion. And her great resolution was built up anew on the bared foundations of her soul.

So, with firm, well measured steps she turned about and wended her way home. It was dark now and a chill wind had crept up. Life looked common-place again; she wondered what romantic fancies had been assailing her that for the time she had lost herself. She felt resolute and strong now; to no one on earth would she ever yield that glorious sense of freedom, independence, *self*-possession.

Just as she approached her own door, a little child toddled into her pathway and stood still. It had wrapt around its tiny figure a woman's shawl, and its quaint little face looked out from the over-large frame of a woman's hat, like a picture in a dark setting.

"I tan't find my Ganma's house," a sweet, plaintive little voice said.

Hagar quickly knelt down and put two loving arms around the lost baby.

"Poor little one! Out in the night all alone! What is your grandma's name?"

"Dess ganma. I put on my mamma's shawl and hat to go call on her."

"What is your name?"

"Pet."

"What is papa's name?"

"Dess papa. Uncle John says 'Dick' to him. I don't. Mamma dess says papa, too."

Hagar reflected a moment still with her arms about the child.

"What work does your papa do?"

"Papa don't work. Plays with Pet, and goes down town."

"To an office or store?"

"Yes. Papa's got lots of horses."

All this did not help Hagar much. Some one would be searching frantically for this child but it was a long way to a police station, and she decided to take her to her own room and see what Esther would advise.

"Will you go home with me while I send some one out to find Ganma or papa?"

"Yes. I like you." And the little girl put her arms confidently around Hagar's neck expecting to be taken up. The soft touch of the little clinging fingers thrilled Hagar as no lover's hand had ever done. She carried her home and startled Esther with her burden, and her own bright, tender face.

"I have found a baby, Esther. Don't you wish we could keep her?"

"A lost baby this time o'day? Poor little thing! I thought you were lost yourself, you were so late. I s'pose somebody's half crazy about the child."

"She says she is called pet, that uncle John calls her papa 'Dick,' and that he keeps lots of horses. Do you know whose she is?" Esther thought a moment.

"Why yes, there's a Mr. Richard Harvey who keeps a large livery stable up town, and lives away out on the other side of the city. I'll put my things and go there right away."

"It is too bad to have you go but it seems necessary."

"Oh I will like it," and away the willing Esther went.

Hagar unwrapped the child and sat down with her in her lap. She was very pretty, her little eyes were quaint and old-fashioned, her breath fanning her cheek was sweet as May flowers. Hagar got some warm milk and bread and fed her then sat smoothing her silky brown hair while the child prattled on in a confiding, fascinating, manner that endeared her every moment more and more. It was two hours before any one came. The little girl lay in Hagar's arms fast asleep, one soft hand clasping her finger, her breath coming and going between the sweet red lips, with all that witchery of childhood and innocence which slumber gives the young. Then the bell rang violently, a man came swiftly up the stairs and after a hurried knock at her door opened and entered. The little girl awoke, called "papa" and in a moment more was in his arms. The man thanked her heartily, expressed his great relief, and pledged to do them any favor or kindness that should ever be in his power. He was gone at last, and Hagar's arms and heart felt strangely empty. The voice of the little one echoed in her ears; her touch, her sweet presence seemed every moment just felt and gone again. Never, since the morning she first knew she had no mother, had she ever felt so inexpressibly lonely.

And what was there *for her*, in life to ever fill this void?

A great longing from this time forth, filled her being—a great longing for a little child all her own.

XV

Women's Appropriate Sphere

In the days that followed Hagar seemed to be in a dream; she scarcely knew how to answer Paul—and she wrote him simply, to wait. Not that he was to cherish any thought of marrying her eventually, but she could not yet say to him what she wished, and just then she wanted to be alone, to have time to think, to understand herself. To Mr. Hathaway she was ready to give an immediate and decided answer when he came for it.

"I thank you and honor you," she said, "for I believe you are offering me what you think is the best and greatest man can offer a woman,—his love, protection, support and name. But I must decline. I could not love you well enough to be your wife—

if I did, I should love you too well to become such. I shall never marry any one."

"You cannot mean that, Miss Lyndon," he said with a confident smile, for he could not believe that a poor working girl, though a very handsome one, could really refuse as eligible a party as himself.

"I do. I never shall marry. Marriage, as I have seen it, has little in it to tempt me. And I feel that I have a work to do in life that I can best do alone."

"But surely, a single life, when it must be full of toil, loneliness, comparative poverty, can not present any attractions. As my wife you should be saved all care, drudgery and struggle; your life would be full of ease and comfort and peace."

"Would you have me marry you without love, to obtain all these advantages?"

A shade of embarrassment passed over the gentleman's face.

"I should hope to win your love, of course. I do not think it would be impossible."

"Many girls marry under just such circumstances; sometimes it turns out as fortunately as other marriages; often the love comes to the woman for someone else when it is too late. Whatever happens they are both bound for life, and that cannot mean happiness for either. People who are not free, cannot long be lovable—bondage kills love sooner or later."

"You talk strangely, Miss Lyndon; I am sure I should never make a slave of you."

"You would not intend to. I do not think as a general thing men are tyrannical husbands because they are *bad*, or cruelly inclined. Many and many a man whose wife is unhappy, would if he *knew*, do and be whatever is required to make her happy. His whole life is built up on custom, the old time rules of religion and law and he does not realize that in any possible way he is invading his wife's rights or restricting her liberty. You, for instance, believe you could safely promise me freedom throughout the future. You can scarcely realize what that may mean. I might desire, for my own happiness, to live apart from you for long periods. I might want a part at least of my home to be sacred to me alone, where no one in the world had a right to intrude uninvited. I might wish to choose my own society, when and where I pleased. If I insisted on these rights you would be hurt and offended. You see, you believe you could guarantee I would not be a bondswoman as your wife, because you are so confident I should never wish to do things you do not like. But you see, no two individuals can always think and desire exactly alike."

"I expect of course you will always be a respectable woman as you are now," the suitor said rather stiffly.

"But we might differ on what constitutes respectability. I might truly love you and still believe that some of these privileges would be conducive to the lasting happiness of both of us. While my sanity remains I do not believe I could ever be false to my own sense of right, but I might do much that would displease you. And I think even at such a risk, I could never consent to give up my own individuality."

"You have some very curious ideas, Miss Lyndon. Really if these are your honest sentiments I should—I should really be afraid to entrust my life's happiness to your keeping——"

"And would congratulate yourself that I had the good sense not to accept your offer," Hagar interrupted with one of her bright, rare smiles. "True, Mr. Hathaway, if your life's happiness depends on my always acting in accordance with your wishes, with the custom of wives in general, you would *not* be safe. That is because you, with other men, do not know any better. You have no faith in a free woman. You do not believe in her power or willingness to make you happy. The best of you believe that some restraint, either of personal control, law, rules of society, is necessary to *make* woman come up to a certain model, in which you imagine your sole chance of happiness lies. You are blind, blind. Wait until the world has seen a generation of free women! That coming, free woman, will teach you a happiness you have never dreamed of! She will show you how beautiful love is! She will show how grand a lover, a worker, a character, a human may become! Being first thoroughly a woman and belonging to herself, she will teach us how much better *every* relation to her fellow beings may be filled, than now. *I* shall never be afraid to trust the happiness of mankind in the hands of free women."

Mr. Hathaway looked at the glowing enthusiastic young face with a man's admiration, not with a bright soul's comprehension. He thought he loved her very much, but vaguely resented the fact that there was so much about her that eluded him, awed him, as before a mystery.

"Indeed, Miss Lyndon, you must excuse me if I cannot see why woman is not as free as she needs to be. Men are not tyrants; they must be strange women indeed, who *want* to do anything more than custom and marriage, as an institution, allows them."

"It is not yet known what a perfectly free woman might *want* to do. I feel safe to trust her to do that which will make the world purer, happier, wiser. Heretofore her goodness or her wrong doing has scarcely been her own affair. She has not been free to test her own character."

"You are beyond me, Miss Lyndon. And since you give me no hope, I may as well leave you. I trust you may never regret your decision."

"Which means that you hope I will. But remember I appreciate the honor you think you have done me and thank you for it. Good bye."

She offered her hand which he hastily pressed, then took his departure as though it were a relief to get away.

Hagar smiled musingly as she looked after him.

"An average man, such as the world calls upright, kind-hearted, good. Yet, he is frightened at the idea that his wife might want to live her own life, be *herself*, in fact, not an appendage."

Madame Anele was very angry when she found that Hagar had refused her relative. She had believed she was doing a great deal for her by helping along the match, for of course a man like Harold Hathaway might easily take his pick among wealthy girls; and Hagar had nothing but the labor of her own hands. What could the girl expect? She could no more comprehend her than could the discarded suitor, and so, for some time she was very distant and cool toward her employee. She was too valuable an assistant to discharge, however, and Hagar kept her place, working away mechanically, her thoughts so pre-occupied she scarcely noticed Madame's air of offended dignity.

Some weeks went by and still the promised letter to Paul had not been written. She heard from him and sent two or three short notes asking still his patience. One day her aunt sent for her—something she had never done before. Hagar hastened to visit her and found her ill, feverish and despondent, and insisted on sending for a physician. His verdict was very discouraging, and Hagar, without asking leave of her employer or of the patient, who would have sent for a hired nurse instead, took up her position at her bedside. Her watch was a sad and tedious one, for there was little hope that her aunt would recover. She seemed not to care to live, and slowly and willingly let go her hold on life. She died peacefully one morning at sunrise.

Hagar grieved for her because she had ever been a true friend; they understood one another, and none knew better what possibilities of lovely womanhood Clive possessed had it not been for the cruelty of society, than Hagar. But she had seen that the world held little happiness for the unfortunate woman, and her sorrow was not despairing. After the funeral when her will was read, it was found that she had left her money to her loved niece. Hagar had never before thought of the money and that she alone was likely to receive it. But when she knew it was her own, a strange, glad, yet serious light came into her eyes and did not leave them.

She did not return to her old situation though Madame Anele repeatedly sent for her. The lady came to see her presently and urged her with peculiar eloquence to enter a partnership with her.

"Your money will not always last without investment," she urged. "I promise you, with your taste, your business ability you can quadruple your capital in a brief, brief time."

But Hagar gently though firmly refused.

"I have something else to do, Madame. This money makes me free and independent. I can live as I want to live—work, hope, think, *act!* It is as though all chains were broken for me. I must live my own life. Pardon me, but I have other views."

Hagar moved into her aunt's house and installed Esther as house keeper. No one could be happier over the change than was this tired woman, for the arrangement allowed her to leave the shop and enjoy a more comfortable and quiet home than she had ever known in her life.

About the time they were well settled in their new home, Hagar received another very urgent letter from Paul. He had been offered a very advantageous position as travelling correspondent, which would take him a long trip through the old world and to some of the eastern countries as yet little visited; he wanted her advice, he would go or stay as she said, and he *must* see her. Surely he could come and visit her now? One word from her was enough.

With a tremor at her heart that would not be stilled Hagar lightly penned the one word "Come."

XVI

Rebelling

Although before she thought there could be time, Paul's name was announced by Esther. It was in the afternoon of a lovely day and Hagar, with a gladness in her expressive face and a light in her dark eyes that made them wonderous, hastened down to meet her old friend.

They clasped hands and for a moment silently gazed at each other. Paul had grown more manly looking, stronger, handsomer than ever, with that grace and ease of manner which comes of true nobility and self-respect. His eyes brightened with surprise and delight. Could this queenly woman with thoughtful brow and deep, lustrous, soulful eyes, be the slim, sallow girl he had known in his youth? He knew her though, for the character and determination in the refined face, and, if he had ever believed beautiful, cultured women could only come of the idle classes, the illusion was now forever dispelled.

They found their voices soon, however, and felt they could scarcely talk fast enough, so much had each to say to the other. Old reminiscences, what had befallen each, their present welfare—all the topics that come up between old friends after a long separation, were touched upon.

Hagar strongly advised Paul to accept the offer which had been made him. She knew the opportunity would afford a chance for the full development of his generous talents, that he could gain a name for himself as well as financial benefit, and receive the advantage of experience and travel. He had three weeks of leisure before he was obliged to start and asked no greater happiness than to spend them near her. He had put up at a quiet hotel in the vicinity, and with delicacy hastened to assure her that no more of her time should be intruded upon than she desired. For several days their afternoons were passed together in walking, talking, reading—learning to know each other over again. They were delighted to find how nearly their minds had grown and expanded in unison; that their opinions were so nearly the same, that that quick sympathy existed between them which enabled each to understand and respond to the other's slightest thought.

They came in one evening from a long walk, when the daylight had faded, and a great moon of burnished silver was magically transforming the every day world into a fairy scene. The hallway was as yet unlighted and at the further end was a deep window inclosing a sort of rustic seat. Slowly, as if the soft radiance drew them, unconsciously to themselves, they passed on to the window and sat down where the light drapery veiled them from the room. It was so still, so beautiful without. They scarcely spoke as with clasped hands they gazed into the mystical night. Paul's gaze fell on the wrapt face beside him; she looked so fair, so wondrously spirit-like in the moonlight; she was like no other woman on earth.

"Oh Hagar!" he breathed softly but passionately, "is it true that you will send me away—alone? *Can* you do it? We could be so happy together—you and I—we seem made for each other. I know you love me—I can feel that in my own deep love for you. Can you be so cruel to us both? Are you still clinging to that old resolution?"

Hagar drew a deep breath, the soft, mystic, dreamy look dropped from her face and she turned it toward him—grave, serious, firm.

"I am still determined that I will never marry. I believe I have a work to do that could not be done were I to foolishly yield to an emotion, however deep. It cannot be true that woman's natural position is what it now is—cramped, dwarfed, subservient. Some way, some time I may help to open a way to free, strong, independent womanhood. But aside from this great purpose of mine—I could not bury our happiness in the grave of marriage. I could not live and know that we could ever be to each other what so many married lovers come to be. I could not bear the bondage, the dying out of all the tendernesses, the romance, the beauty of our free, youthful love."

"Do not imagine such terrible possibilities—let us accept happiness when it is offered us, fearing not what the future may bring. You shall *be* free—nothing on earth shall ever induce me to restrict your liberty in the least. We want each other; we know how to love, how to be happy. It is not wise to thrust away the bliss so close to us."

"So many lovers have talked thus before. Almost every couple that marries, vows that their happiness shall never be marred by the heartaches, the misunderstandings, that are the lot of others; and yet, but a few years and the same troubles and irritations have ruined their bliss. There is something in the close intimacy of marriage which destroys this chivalrous, generous, respectful spirit that pervades a lover's being and which makes us so happy. Health, freedom, love, peace, seem to die in the atmosphere of that exclusive and intrusive nearness. I could not bear that our mutual feelings should ever be destroyed—I would rather die. I do love you dearly. I *believe* I must always love you; as you are now, I must. If you are absent, I must. But, should I live *with* you, in that close relationship which custom, law and religion enjoin, in which one is certain to be subservient to the other—I could not promise to love you two years hence. You are going away and you will win name, position and competence if you are free to struggle for them. Go, as free as you came—only I know you will think of me with the same love and respect you hold for me now."

"And you are determined to live always alone, loverless, husbandless, childless?"

Paul looked down at her almost sternly—he was growing angry with this beautiful fanatic. She met his gaze—her great dark eyes radiant with deep feeling, steadfastly until their yearning, mysterious depths brought the tears to his own eyes.

"I cannot Paul,"—slowly and softly she spoke, "I cannot live forever, childless."

He drew her toward him reverently. "What would you, my darling? I am yours—yours entirely. You are my queen—in the realm of love mine it is to obey."

She bowed her head upon his breast and with his arms folded tenderly, solemnly about her, she wept. This good, good man did not misunderstand her. To him she was as pure, as lofty, as true a woman as she had ever been—she could never be aught else. Her woman's right to motherhood under her own conditions he never for one moment disclaimed.

Holding her closely, reverently thus, he warned her of sufferings to come; of sorrows the world would inflict that he could not bear for her; of persecutions and misrepresentations that afar off he could not turn aside; he told her that a word from her at any time would call him back from the further most quarters of the earth if she still insisted that he must go. With only a word or two for she was too much moved to talk she assured him of her determination, then begged him to leave her for that night.

———————

The day came for Paul's departure. He was much the sadder of the two, he clung to her as though he could not tear himself away. Arguments and persuasions had had no influence over this strange, sweet, wilful nature.

"I want to be alone, I will be happier alone. I do not accept the bonds you place upon yourself—I pledge nothing for myself, but you shall always be my dear, dear friend. I will know how to reach you if I ever want you. Now go, dear Paul, and oh! I shall miss you." And with that last womanly cry, the tears in her voice, she left him.

The days went quietly by in Hagar's cosy home. She worked, studied, wrote, for she was beginning to send the result of her thoughts to various liberal magazines and papers, and took long walks into the country. Often her face assumed a dreamy, far away look; at times she started suddenly and gazed into space with an expression of awe; or her eyes filled with a strange happiness that was half fear. But never was she for one moment sad or down-cast or abashed. One day she had a long talk with Esther Copeland. Esther betrayed surprise—there were even tears in her eyes before the interview ended, but at its close she clasped Hagar's hand and fervently exclaimed, "I will stick to you through everything, Hagar Lyndon. You may depend on me."

They concluded to move to the country. Hagar longed for the woods and fields, the pure air, the quiet and seclusion of rural life. And in a few weeks a pretty rose-embowered cottage was secured not far from the city, in a lovely, quiet place, and there the two women made their home.

XVII

Fallen

And then Hagar entered upon a quiet domestic life that suited her inclinations in every way. She took long walks on pleasant days, deep into the heart of the woods, where tree and shrub and scented air and song of birds spoke courage to her soul as no human being could; she exercised doing various household duties, always stopping far short of actual weariness; read, studied, wrote when her brain was clearest, and indulged in long, luxuriant peaceful rests whenever she felt the need of rest; she surrounded herself with beautiful pictures and good books, partook of luxuries the rich often forget to give themselves,—pure air, wholesome food and baths of various description. A grand, beautiful, healthful creature she was—such as the future coming woman should aspire to be. As winter approached the walks had to be shortened but were never entirely given up. Otherwise the dark months saw no change in her habits.

The spring with its glad, soft breezes of promise, found her well and content—though very much alone. For Hagar, during her last walk through the streets of her home of several years, found that she had no friends left except among the children. Who among them could understand this determined young woman who would not enter into what she considered a bondage, but *would* take her natural, woman's right at all hazards? Not one. No one can sting a sister woman as a strictly *virtuous* woman can. No one can inflict punishment for errors against society as can respectable wives who are not happy, and who never forgive a lapse from the straight and narrow road they are miserable in. And so Hagar found she must walk her pathway alone.

It happened that near her home there dwelt that unusual sort of personage—a sensible physician; a man whom no one could humbug, wheedle or cajole; who said what he pleased and seldom had people take offense at it; who delighted in getting patients off his hands and so gave good advice, pure water and fresh air and fed them on sweetened water and bread pills when they insisted on being dosed. One day in early summer, this Doctor Hale, was inveigled into Madame Anele's reception room under the pretence that one of the children was slightly ailing. Several influential ladies, "some of the best people of the city" were present, a sort of well-bred, disdainful, half-veiled curiosity pervading their bearing.

"Oh, tell us, Dr. Hale," demurely questioned Madame Anele after he had looked at the child and sent her away to play, "how is my former employee, Miss Lyndon? Naturally I feel a pitying interest in her."

"Who? Oh yes, the lady who was once doing business with you. Oh, she's well."

"Well? We heard she was ill."

"Mrs. Lyndon is one of those sensible people who starve the doctors and never get sick."

"He calls her *Mrs.* Lyndon," said one of the ladies to her neighbor, in a wondering whisper. "It isn't possible—eh?"

Dr. Hale possessed quick ears as well as quick wits.

"Well she is a full-grown, mature woman and has a right to distinguish herself from a school girl if she chooses. A woman need not wait until she is so unfortunate as to marry, to change her childish title—men don't."

"I never heard of a *single* woman calling herself '*Mrs.*,' but Hagar Lyndon always was singular. So, she's well," continued Madame Anele musingly.

"Yes, a little delicate perhaps, but, on the whole, quite well."

"But, Doctor—isn't there—isn't there—a child?"

"Yes, there is. A little beauty—strong, healthy, perfect. I wish you good christian mothers would ever call on me to such good purpose."

"Oh, Doctor!" and "Whyee, Doctor!" and "You are positively shocking!" came in a chorus from these pillars of society.

"Why, what have I said? Let any one of you show me a child welcomed, born of loving, healthy parents, whose mother knows how to take care of herself, and I'll show you another such a beauty. Such a child is truly 'well born,' an aristocrat among babies."

"You can say that of a child born like hers? Who inherits nothing but shame and disgrace?" the eldest, most severe and most substantial lady in the room questioned with shocked face.

"Humbug!" was the doctor's sole answer which so astounded the speaker she had nothing further to say.

"I must say for her," said Madame Anele, "that I never was more shocked and astonished in my life than when I discovered Hagar Lyndon was a ruined woman. She seemed so strong and self-possessed, and carried herself with such courtesy and reserve toward everyone. She was the last young woman in town I would ever imagine could fall. But you can never tell by appearances."

"It's my opinion she never did 'fall,' and she certainly does not look 'ruined' in any sense that I can perceive. She is an independent, self-supporting woman and I presume had prejudices against being a married one, for which I don't blame her if she has lived with her eyes open. And being fully capable of rearing and caring for a child, she has assumed the responsibility, and I don't know, since society is not likely to be burdened, that it is any of society's business. But I must leave you, ladies, to discuss this affair among yourselves."

More than one of the ladies present were vastly interested and would gladly have gone to see Hagar if any plausible excuse could have been found. Had she been poor and low, they could have intruded themselves on her, willing or unwilling, in the character of missionary visitors. If she had been dangerously ill, they could have satisfied their curiosity under cover of Good Samaritanism; but being independent, in quite good health, and lady-like, no tinge of patronage could be given to a call. To visit her at all was to countenance her disgraceful conduct, and church-going wives and mothers could never do that.

But Hagar did not miss them—as yet. On the altars of her home, a shrine had been built, and before it, she and her one true friend were daily worshipers. The small god was a constant wonder. She kissed its pink soft skin, on cheek, brow, lips and hands, and gazed in awed rapture and surprise; that tiny, lovely creature was part of herself. Surely every birth is a miraculous conception.

Everything necessary to be done for the child, was a religious rite at which she and the elder lady were high priestesses. And in the performance of these mystic ceremonies, in adoration and quiet happiness, Hagar almost forgot the world. She wrote to Paul Deane only at long intervals, and then briefly with a shyness that told him little. Paul's answers she hardly allowed herself to read, but kept them near her heart to be vaguely happy over; she dared not think of him too often.

So for two or three months Hagar lived on in the same quiet, seclusion, happy in ministering to the beautiful child who thrived wonderfully under the sole care of the two loving women. But as time passed, her natural vigor and activity made her long for a wider scope for her capabilities; her still, isolated life without acquaintances or absorbing occupation, began to create a vague restlessness within her, though she would scarcely own to herself that she felt a lack. Her child grew dearer every day of his life, but the very fact created a longing to be up and doing some great work for him. He slept, wakened, ate, laughed and crowed so healthily that his care was comparatively nothing. She occasionally wrote, but to one of her nature, action, contact with the bustling, blundering, suffering world, was actually necessary

to stimulate her powers. She must *see* the things she would work

for, know by observation and experience what people suffered

or she could not do her best. Now and then a poetic sketch—a

little airy flower breathing fancy was sent out and accepted, but

this Hagar did not consider as serious work. She needed action,

strong, hard work—something worthy her wonderful energy,

glorious health and mental vigor. Nothing seemed to open before

her, there was no necessity that she should toil for a living,

and for some time Hagar waited, in doubt as to what use the

world had for her, or how she could impress her own ideas and

independence on the class which most needed her example. She

was debating in her mind whether she ought not to see Madame

Anele, invest some money in her business and plunge into active

work once more, when an incident occurred which showed her

how difficult it would be for her to find again a place in the busy

world, as she had hoped to do. She scarcely realized what a gulf

she had made between herself and other energetic, busy women,

but she was soon to be made to feel it.

XVIII

Cast Out from Society

It was one of those soft warm days that sometimes comes very late in the fall like a wafted good bye from summer; the doors of Hagar's little home were wide open to let in the perfumed air, and she herself stood at one of the long windows gazing dreamily out on the golden-tinted landscape. A lady and child drove by in a basket phaeton, slowly, the lady gazing about her in a hesitating manner as though undecided where to go; finally she drew up to the gate, alighted and came up the flower-bordered walk.

"Excuse me," she began politely, as after a light rap she saw a woman coming towards her; "excuse me, but could you tell me where————good heavens!"

Hagar had caught up her child as she passed from the window to the hall door and stood before the lady with it in her arms.

"Mercy! Did any one see me coming in here?" and the lady looked around with apparent great anxiety. "I think not—it is a quiet neighborhood."

"What did you wish to know, Mrs. Rivers?"

Hagar recognized the lady as one of Madame Anele's customers, and answered with calm dignity.

"I would not ask anything of such a woman as you are!" the woman sputtered, growing red in the face. "How can you stand there and look me in the face with that child in your arms without dying of shame? How can you breathe the air in my presence and not burn up with blushes? A girl with every chance and every inducement to remain honorable and respectable, you deliberately chose vice and disgrace. I wonder that such as you are allowed to hold up their heads in the same neighborhood with virtuous girls. You ought to be———"

"Madame, did you come her to insult me? Leave my house!" Hagar advanced with cheeks glowing and eyes flashing.

"Leave *your* house indeed! You should get down on your knees that I honored your house———"

But Hagar came so close, with such a grand indignation burning in her face, that the visitor retreated suddenly.

Hagar's excitement lasted until the woman was fairly out of the yard, and then she walked feebly to the sofa in the parlor. She grew white and cold and her lips trembled; she felt as though she had received stinging blows from a whip. A woman—a stranger could come into her house and say such things to her! She felt a sudden terror of the world—a wild impulse to fly with her child to some wilderness where no one would ever find her. If all people were like this woman she was not safe among them. But where could she go? What could she do? Never, until this moment had she realized with what vengeance society punishes those who break her laws. She had been neglected and shunned and old acquaintances and friends had turned from her coldly; but she had been preoccupied and interested, and had scarcely noticed the lack their neglect left in her life. Now when her whole being was waking from its sweet, secluded spell, and her faculties were clamoring for a more extended sphere, she was suddenly brought face to face with knowledge of the gulf between herself and her old position. But after a time—when she fully recovered from the shock, she found her courage renewed. A new defiance, a self-reliance, a complete confidence in her own powers, seemed to spring up within her; she determined on a new course. She would go out more, she would show people that she was *not* ashamed, that she was as pure and good, as strong and useful a woman as ever she had been. She knew there must be work for her among women who were more unhappy than she—who were poor and persecuted and above all—weighed down by a consciousness of degradation.

No woman with health, strength, ability and willingness need ever consider herself ruined, and this great truth she would teach her sisters. She could seek out these unfortunate women, she could write, she could talk, could even make speeches if necessary. So in this new spirit she thought and studied and laid plans for the future, finding herself becoming deeply interested, and learning that life needs to be wider than one's own little home, one's own loves and immediate surroundings.

But she was yet to experience more of the annoyances and trials of her peculiar position. Before she could put any of her plans into operation, she received another call. This time it was from a man—her landlord. He had no occasion to see her, as all business had been transacted through an agent at the city office, but he said with a great attempt at gallant politeness, that he wished to know his tenant better, to learn if there was anything he could change, anything he could add to the place, that would enhance her comfort. He was a large, pompous man, unused to the little courtesies of life, and his awkward endeavors to be gallant and attractive, sat very illy upon his ungainly person. Hagar very coldly informed him that there was nothing he could do for her, that there was no business whatever which would

require his attention, and then waited for him to take his leave.
But this he had no intention of doing. He talked of the weather,
the place, the prospects of the country, despite Hagar's short and
chilly answers, until, tired from his unusual efforts he finally
departed, with a smile meant to be fascinating enough to inspire
an invitation to call again. Hagar feared that was not the last of
him, and she was right.

Much of Hagar's sincere efforts to do something for her
suffering sisters must be lightly passed over, as the details of such
a work would form a book of themselves. As is usual, when one
expects to benefit a class one knows very little about, Hagar
made many blunders, met with many rebuffs, found herself often
looked upon as a meddler, and often laid herself liable to insults
and misrepresentations.

The young are enthusiastic, and do not learn until long
after many repeated failures and heart-burnings, that a mere
desire to benefit humanity is not sufficient preparation for doing
so. A novice invariably patronizes, meddles, fails to enter into
the spirit or conditions of the people to be helped. One must
make themselves *one* of the class they would aid, feel as they feel,
suffer as they suffer, love them, confide in them, and then be
sufficiently studied in the true relations of mankind to each other
to form some kind of an idea of a remedy, before any great good

can be done. Hagar had much to learn before her best work was to be done.

Enough to relate, that after many discouragements she succeeded in gaining the confidence of one poor woman, of inspiring her with a little self-respect, of setting her to work, and getting her to promise to tell her of other cases which might come to her knowledge. Then she devoted herself more to writing. At the same time, her greatest happiness consisted in caring for, in loving, and watching the growth of her beautiful babe. It almost became a question of dispute between herself and Esther, who fairly worshiped him, which should care for him the most. But through all the days, a restlessness, a vague want haunted her, disturbed her content and sometimes faintly suggested the thought that after all—was she entirely right? What needed she—a free, independent, self-supporting, vigorous woman, to complete her happiness?

And then, too, the difficulties which a woman in her situation must expect to encounter, began to multiply.

XIX

Outside the Pale of Society

A lady called one day whose appearance was very striking and impressive; she was elegantly dressed, spoke in a well-bred manner, possessed a self-assured air, and, while seeming never to be abashed, was not over bold. Hagar wondered, when she first introduced herself, if some influential member of the "best circles" had not come to befriend and encourage her; but her quick intuitions soon told her that idea was a mistake; the visitor talked in a vague and general way, and for some time Hagar could not comprehend toward what her finely turned phrases were leading. But at last it dawned upon her.

It seemed that the woman owned an elegant and quiet establishment in the city—everything connected with it was of the most refined, exclusive type, but she wished a partner. She had heard of Hagar—she could guarantee wealth, leisure, happiness, ease. Hagar's money was not mentioned, but no doubt in the lady's mind it figured largely.

At first Hagar could not speak. The blood slowly surged to her face until it burned like fire. She felt a deeper sense of resentment—of having received a deadly insult than when the society lady had stung her with reproaches and epithets. That such a woman should *dare* think of her in connection with herself and her calling! Could it be *possible*, that any one—any one on the round earth, even among the most conservative, could see anything in common between her and this woman? She arose without speaking and walked to the window; the color left her cheeks, and her face grew pale and set.

"You have understood me, Miss Lyndon?" the visitor said, inquiringly, with a manner just slightly tinged with embarrassment.

Hagar was thinking. She saw more clearly than ever before how people looked upon a woman who had done what she had; she realized that the world would naturally class this woman of the public, and herself together. Then she saw that in her own mind the old prejudices had not been cleared away, or why should she think of this person as a being whose very speech was a degradation and an insult? She was a woman—perhaps there was much that was good in her, and surely she was capable of great usefulness. There was no reason why she should not talk quietly and rationally with her.

"You have mistaken me completely," she said, turning around at last. "You should not have come to me with such an offer."

"I meant no offense," the lady said uneasily, "of course you understand that in the position I offer you, you would be free—you would not be influenced—that is—there are others—"

"You misunderstand me, I repeat. I presume you take your cue from the tone of society about you, and I ought not to be indignant at you personally. But *try*, Madame, to comprehend that I have never lost my self-respect. I am a free woman, I have never given a man a look, a word, a caress that was not natural and true. I did not wish to become a wife, but I have an inherent right to be a mother; I have brought no burdens upon any one—my child is healthy, beautiful, intelligent and I am able financially and physically to care for him. Do you imagine that any thing on earth could induce *me*—who have braved *so much* to belong solely to myself—to become the kind of a slave you invite me to become?"

The stranger stared at her, but had no words to offer. Hagar continued after a moment of silence.

"You know *you* are not free. I am. My love, or esteem, or any expression of those feelings, could only be won by the worthiest and best. You are constrained by love of gain or other outside influences to do that from which your spirit often recoils; yet, you might free yourself. You have not an ordinary face—you might get out of this slavery if you chose. True, the woman who sells herself either in marriage or out of it naturally outrages her own humanity and as a result sinks, or retrogrades; but while any strength, or vitality, or desire to rise, exists within her, she is never 'ruined.' If she persists in living only to excite and pander to abnormal passions, she must necessarily become degraded. But you look too strong, too intelligent to persist in such a course. You are wronging the women whom you lead into your employ, when you might instead do them good. You have no bonds to break, no superstitious links to sever; why do you not leave such a life? You, well to do, impressive, independent, could step into a better and higher field today if you wished; you could aid woman instead of helping to destroy her."

The woman, sitting while Hagar stood, did not look up as she answered with a perturbed effort at lightness.

"You are preaching, Miss Lyndon. If you understood the subject at all, you would know there *are* barriers against my dropping my present method of life, and turning—missionary. It would not do. In real life saints are not made in a twinkling of sinners."

"You can easily *start* on a different course."

"Not so easily. Where among honorable women could I find a place?"

"That is hard to do, I own, but—say you cannot find a place with 'honorable women,' there is still much happiness, great chances for usefulness, left you. You understand unfortunate women better than most of those who seek sincerely to save them. You would know how to approach them, how to gain their confidence, how to set them on the better pathway."

"You are setting me a task you know little about, Miss Lyndon. While society is as it is, while conditions remain as they are, and men are the creatures they are, there will be women like myself, there will be a fascination about our lives we find hard to resist, an impossibility in our assuming the lives of respectable women."

"But it is the part of woman to lead the race upward; she must come up from the depths—men will advance."

The woman laughed unpleasantly, "Oh, well, you are getting beyond me. I expected to find you a listener, and here I am being preached into something like seriousness—a state of mind I never continue in long. I acknowledge you have treated me kindly, your advice is well meant and I like you, though I don't understand you, I'm sure. But I fear you cannot impress me," and she gathered up her rich cape about her shoulders and rose to go. Hagar looked at her a little sadly. "I am afraid the world has not fitted you to understand me. You could do so much good. I tremble to think of the sorrow you may cause, instead."

"I believe in your sincerity, Miss Lyndon," she said as though for a moment really touched. "But it's of no use. The world would not let me live any other way if I wished. I don't see how it allows *you* to live independently and purely. Good bye," and in a moment more she was gone.

The visit left Hagar in a sad, reflective mood which lingered for some time. But it was not the last or the least of her annoyances. The land lord came again. He made no pretension of business and tried more than before to make himself especially agreeable. Hagar's coldness made no impression upon him, for before he left he managed to make occasion to offer her the place, rent free, together with many other luxuries, if "she would place herself under his protection."

Hagar ordered him to leave the house and called Esther to see that he obeyed. His real brutality showed itself as he glared back at her from the path.

"Ah! my fine lady, you'll be sorry for this! Trying to set up for virtuous with that brat in your arms! You'll be sorry!"

Esther slammed the door and double-locked it. Hagar was just sinking helplessly into a hall seat.

"Great Heavens, Esther! Must I endure such things as this forever? Have I given people any excuse—any reason on earth, to come into my home as they have and attack me and insult me? Am I safe no where?"

"Oh my dear, dear Miss Lyndon, if I could save you from it all, I would. I'll let no one inside this door again until I'm *sure* they're friends. I'm afraid you didn't count on the cruelty of the world, dear. Men are such brutes—I mean so many of 'em are. If they think that a woman is the least bit free of the customs of society or don't feel bound by laws and priests, she is fair plunder to any of 'em. They think that is all that keeps women straight and they can do as they like with 'em. If they're refused they're mad and revengeful. They're not fit to know good women—they can't possibly be brought to understand 'em."

"Esther, I'm beginning to be afraid of my kind. Let us leave this place. I *can't* live in that man's house a day longer. Let us go to a large city, where we can live our own lives unmolested, better than here."

"I am willing. And I'm sure it will be better for us all. I foresee nothing but trouble for you here, and brave as you are, dear girl, it will break you down sooner or later. How fortunate you are not poor and dependent on these spiteful people!"

"Baby would then have been impossible."

"Wouldn't your father have helped you?"

Hagar thought of Clive's fate.

"No indeed. He would be the worst among them. Even Lucy has never answered my letters since *he* came. I suppose they have forbidden her to have anything to do with me."

X X

The Legal Protection of a Name

So Hagar and Esther decided to change their residence again.
Hagar long since had determined that she would never pass as
a widow to save herself annoyance, for she was not ashamed of
her motherhood. It was not, therefore, that she might disguise
her identity that she wished for a new home, but that her
identity might not be a matter of so much importance to every
one around. In a large city people are too plentiful to allow of
minute inquiry into the details of every one's life; for one thing,
nobody cares. This lack of sympathy and interest sometimes
chills the ruralist newly come into a city, but in time he becomes
used to the apparent neglect and finds that it is not so much

a lack of human sympathy as it is a stronger development of individuality—the disposition to let every body manage their own lives—yet the sympathy comes usually, when there is a genuine call for it.

After many little annoyances which it is not necessary to relate in detail, Hagar and Esther with their little charge found themselves established in a pleasant flat in a well-to-do neighborhood. Nearly all of her vexations were because of her peculiar position, she found. Expressmen were impudent and stubborn; men whom she had to hire to do necessary work were disrespectful and slow. And finally when she come to rent a place, she saw that agents and owners were reluctant to deal with a lonely woman accompanied by a child and nurse, who would not say she was a widow, or give any satisfactory information concerning her husband. Wearily at last she settled down in her tasteful and comfortable home, and hoped to be happy.

Why she was not as the days went by, she could scarcely have told. Whether her nerves were more sensitive, or whether experience had taught her what to look for, it seemed to her that she had constantly to be steeling herself against disrespect, annoyances, insults, or on the other hand, unwelcome and over-bold admiration. Strong and self-possessed as she naturally was, this wore upon her, until she found herself weakened and illy fitted for work or close application to any occupation. She had no companionship except that of Esther, no friends, no congenial spirits to encourage and stimulate her own. Try as she would she could not at all times control her own loneliness and restlessness.

And deep in her heart dwelt an intense longing to see Paul. She would not listen to it—would not heed it for an instant—but there it was, smothered perhaps, but clamoring, clamoring for recognition. She would fly to her boy and in the smiles of his dimpled, rosy face, the clasp of his velvety little hands, forget for a time and be happy. But this could not last, and it was with dismay and surprise she had to acknowledge to herself that her baby could not fill her life and make her entirely content.

A letter from Paul would set her heart fluttering so that it terrified her. She would not read it at all for hours, sometimes days, because, she discovered, it made her *too* happy.

"I must never, never see him again," she said to herself. "I could not send him away again if I should. And he has proved himself so good, so true, so loving—I fear I *must* love him too well. I will not ruin our lives by marrying—alas! what *shall* I do with him if he ever comes to me? What shall I do with my traitoress self? He must never find me, never. He does not know yet where I am, and one is so easily lost in a great city."

And a sad echo within her being, sighed again, "so easily lost."

Sometimes Hagar attended on Sunday afternoons, the lectures of a man, who had left the orthodox church, but who had carried with him a large following, and much of the poetic ceremony of his old associations. He was eloquent, his utterances were idealistic and soothing and Hagar became deeply interested in his discourses. He was a plain, middle-aged man, he had never married, and in private life was shrinking, unassuming—embarrassed with a shyness of which no public work had ever cured him. Hagar one day wished very intensely for an explanation to some passage which had seemed obscure and yet which had deeply interested her. She lingered after the meeting was over, hoping for an opportunity to speak a few words to him. It was an unusual thing for Hagar to do in these days—seeking to speak unaddressed to a stranger—but she was in one respect *an intellect*—a mind seeking communication with another mind—forgetting sex (and indeed it does not in reality exist in the intellect, difference being the result of conditions, heredity, environments) and wishing only for light. Of course the gentleman was surrounded for some time, and it was only that his eye chanced to light on her, lingering outside the circle alone, that the opportunity was given her. As soon as he conveniently could, he broke way from the others and approached her. He offered his hand timidly and said hesitatingly,

"Do I know you? Do you wish to speak to me?"

His very diffidence gave her courage. "You do not know me at all," she said with one of her rare, beautiful smiles; "But I have had the pleasure of listening to you frequently and am deeply interested. I have followed your arguments and propositions very closely but I want more light on the subject treated today. Will you explain what you meant by this:

"Let us not worship the unknown but declare war against it—let us conquer it, there is nothing unknowable—a philosophy which ends in the unknowable, is like a badly stated problem that never comes out right."

"My dear young lady," the lecturer said evidently ill at ease, I never know what I meant in an address ten minutes after it is delivered. I was probably quoting or plagiarizing. By the middle of the week I shall be clear headed again. Some of my flock, inquirers, strangers, any one interested may visit my study Wednesday evenings. Would you care to come then?"

Hagar intuitively shrank back; then she thought, why should she hesitate? If she met others so much the better; she could meet them on an intellectual plane and they need not know her story, or care anything about her personality. It would open the way to the mental stimulus she was craving.

She went on the evening named, and found herself very glad that she had done so. She met two or three intellectual people there, who received her cordially and to whom she listened with great pleasure. She saw that she could hold her own with them, that they heard her with attention and respectful admiration as she with quiet dignity expressed her own thoughts. The lecturer seemed peculiarly attracted to her. He blushed like a girl when he spoke to her, and yet seemed charmed into doing so as often as possible. She appeared to him so unusual a being—a beautiful woman seemingly without consciousness of her beauty, bright, mentally and physically strong, calm, self-possessed, reserved. To know her thoroughly he thought must be a great happiness, yet he felt that the mind which frankly met his own would be all he would ever know. Her life, her emotions, her feelings, were folded away from the outer world, he felt certain.

And yet the acquaintance so quietly begun, continued until quite a degree of friendship had grown up between the two and he had ventured to call on her. He had not learned anything of her life, her position or her circumstances though he had studied her character, intellect, and the strange winsome charm of her presence quite thoroughly. When he called, her baby boy was in the room with her.

"This is my boy; isn't he beautiful? You know one must say that to be friends with me," she said laughingly as she took him up.

Mr. Daniel Wyng looked at her quickly, and most assuredly turned a shade paler than was natural.

"Your own? Ah! then, you are married—you are not *Miss* Lyndon?"

Hagar looked straight into his eyes and said quietly but firmly,

"This is my son. But, I am not married, Mr. Wyng."

He gazed, startled and silenced, into her dark, lustrous eyes for a full minute. Then he recalled himself with something like a sob.

"Ah! Pardon me—I do not mean to be curious—to intrude into your personal sorrows—"

"You have not intruded; I meant you should know if you ever became interested enough to care."

"You have been unfortunate then. Some one deceived you. You were never to blame, Miss Lyndon, I could swear to your purity, your face is the face of a good, true woman."

"I thank you kindly, Mr. Wyng. I do not consider myself a false or a bad woman."

"Then some one wronged you terribly. Miss Lyndon, will you tell me your story? If you have no friend, no brother—let *me* be your avenger. Let me bring your betrayer to justice."

"What would you do? How could you bring him to justice?"

"I would search the world over for him, I would bring him to your feet, I would not rest until he had legally given you his name."

"Would you have me marry him if he has deceived and wronged me so?"

For an instant a flash of indignation, of rebellion against such a thought flitted across the good man's features.

"What else could I do? What else could he do to right you?"

"He could let me alone. Mr. Wyng, if a man ever had deceived, betrayed and then deserted me, *I would not marry him.* I would not trust my whole future, give my whole self to a man who had done all in his power to make me unhappy."

"Then there was some mistake. The man died perhaps too soon to right you—there was a false ceremony for which no one was to blame, Miss Lyndon, if this is so, I—I will set you right before the world, I, if you will——"

"There, there, Mr. Wyng, go no further. You can scarcely know what you are saying to a woman almost a stranger. I am the victim of no mistake, no deceit, no wrong of any kind. My child's father is one of the noblest men that ever lived. I did not wish to marry because marriage as it exists makes slaves of women and is the grave of love and happiness of both men and women. I longed to become a mother and I possessed the natural right to motherhood, being healthy, financially independent, and fairly intelligent. I simply chose to exercise it."

My Wyng's breath seemed fairly taken away. "You astound me. I do not know what to say—I cannot understand you."

"Then do not try. I will excuse you if you wish to go."

"You deliberately chose suffering, ignominy——"

"I did not *choose*, but I have suffered." Hagar looked weary and touchingly sad as she said this.

"Miss Lyndon, I cannot hide it even from myself. I love you, and if you *will* be my wife——"

"No, no—you, popular, respected, great—you must not say such words to me. You are carried away by emotion and sympathy. Go now and think seriously, then see if you would say the same."

XXI

The Unequal Struggle

The ex-minister at first seemed disposed to insist on an answer; but Hagar gave him her hand and said good bye in so decided a manner he had no alternative but to go. It might have occurred to him that he was acting quite hastily and that it would be better to meditate in solitude before he took such a reckless step, but whether or no, he bowed and with a significant, "you will see me again, Miss Lyndon," hurriedly departed.

"Only when I see you on the rostrum," Hagar said softly as the door closed behind him. She smiled, a little sadly perhaps, for she did not believe him so noble a man as to be in earnest when once he had time to reflect. She had by this time grown used to the world.

A few days passed and the gentleman did not call again; but something happened that thrilled Hagar as nothing he might do, ever would. Paul wrote that he was coming home—even by the time his letter should be in her hands, he would have landed. He asked her to write immediately and tell him where to find her as he must see her—once at least, and he could not wait in suspense very long. For once Hagar was simply a girl, and sat down and cried over the letter. She wept for him, for herself, for their future, while her heart was throbbing with a secret joy that he was so near—so near, once more. At last she "gathered up her forces"—called up all the strength of her strong character and resolved there must be no more of that foolish sentimentality. She wrote to him, but it was to say that she could not see him yet— that he must wait indefinitely, that sometime she would send for him as one friend might for another, but *that* she could not do just yet. This letter sent on its way, she felt more calm. But by the time an answer might be expected, she was in a state of feverish, anxious restlessness again. What would he say? Would he leave it to her decision, and go his own way until they should both forget? She tried to picture Paul as the husband of some other woman—his life filled with loves and duties in which she had no part. It gave her a quick, involuntary pang of anguish, and then—

it was as though her soul smiled in calm, superior confidence—
and something said, "He loves *me*. He can have no life of which I
am not a part. Though he have other loves and other duties, I am
a part of himself—he loves me."

A little later than expected the letter came. It was long, it
was like Paul, it was almost as though he held her in his arms and
whispered these words to her:

"Dearest: I know it is not your heart that
speaks when you bid me not to come to you; I have
no need to appeal to that. You think your reason
dictates this course, and to that I answer, using, not
my feelings, not my passionate longing, but my best,
coolest judgment.

I have observed, I have read and thought and
reasoned in the year and a half that I have been
absent from you. I see more clearly than I used,
why you object so strongly to marriage as a legal
institution. I know that in form it is but a relic
of barbaric ages when for generations the woman
was bought and paid for, or fought for, conquered
and carried off as prisoner. The institution of
today is veiled with a rosy film in which womanly
duty, chastity, modesty, obedience to God and the
husband, flit like silvery dream-clouds, hiding the

actual, hard, cold chains, or rather, taking their
place, since they hold the soul of woman as tightly
as did the more rigid ones of old. I know that a
terrible blight seems to rest on all humanity from
this very curse; it kills love and tenderness, respect
and kindness, romance and beauty; it dwarfs
the bodies and souls of children. It brings them
unwelcomed into a cruel world; it degrades the
mothers and makes outcasts of those who are not
wives. It has repressed the *woman spirit* until we have
a civilization almost without the feminine element—
and what a monstrosity it is! Full of cruelty and
murder, of authority, force and repression, of
wanton lavishness and horrible want and hunger,
of criminal idleness and miserable drudgery. Yes,
Hagar, I acknowledge all you have ever said of
marriage, and arraign it even stronger. But in doing
so I do not forget that men and women are made for
each other. They need one another's companionship,
love, encouragement, magnetism, inspiration.
Because we disapprove of the institution of marriage
as established by our mistaken civilization and
supported by the authority of church and state,
it is no reason that men and women should make

martyrs of themselves, renounce one another and
live alone, unhappy and dissatisfied. Men and
women of intellect with the cobwebs of superstition
and prejudice brushed from their minds, surely can
be trusted to adjust their relations to each other so as
to exclude the inharmonies that result from ordinary
marriages. I believe you and I can. And now let me
tell you wherein you are wrong, and why people
who are freed from the old conventionalities, may
still consistently marry in the societary sense. You
have been more brave, more noble in living up to
your convictions and bearing all the consequences
uncomplainingly alone, than any woman I have
ever known or ever expect to know. *But you wrong
yourself and you wrong your child by taking up an
unequal struggle in which no one can aid you.* You
have no more right, if you believe in equal freedom,
to wrong yourself than to wrong another. If the
consequences of a rebellion against the laws of
religion, government and society, could be borne by
the man and woman concerned *equally*, they would
be justified in such rebellion. But that is impossible.
Do you not see that a man placed in my position
with a heart full of love and longing, his whole being

filled with a yearning to shield the woman he loves and share her burdens, can do nothing but stand aside in ease and safety, while the world flings its arrows and stings at *her?* Suppose the man in such a case were not well-intentioned, were unreliable, swayed by impulse and self-interest. Granted, a woman would be unhappy with him under any circumstances; but today she can leave him if she has been legally married and take up life as honored and respected as before. There was a time only a few years ago when she could not do this. If there is no legal tie she bears all the burdens, all the ignominy and disgrace while society receives him as kindly as before. If two people could defy society on an equal footing it would be right for them to do so, if they wished. But as things are, they can not. She alone must receive the scorn of society; as a consequence she must brave poverty, loneliness, and bear the responsibility of the children that may come to her. If a mutual agreement is entered into to last as long as both wish and is afterward dissolved, only the woman suffers. Her life as far as her relations with her fellow beings is concerned, is ruined. She cannot commence where she left off, when she met him. *He can.*

Free women under just economic conditions would no doubt prefer to provide for their own children rather than compel the assistance of an unwilling father. But none of us are free yet and there are no just economic conditions; women have a double burden to bear, an unequal struggle to wage when they have no legal claim on the father of their children. It is not a fair fight; and until better conditions can be secured, women should not take upon themselves so one-sided a war. They may work for woman's emancipation, for their right to own themselves, for freedom from all their many hoary old bondages; but let us not ask her to bear the punishments for the sins of all humanity—to suffer all the pangs of a race regenerating itself.

Let us speak of ourselves. Your course has been actuated by the purest, highest principle. There was no strong, passionate influence on one side, no weak yielding on the other. Our love has been as mutual, as free, as equal as love can be at this stage of the world's progress. You are free, yet your mother love has met response. And yet, oh my darling! I know

you have paid dearly for your freedom and I, with
an aching heart, am powerless to help you.

Men and women honor me. I am allowed to
earn a living easily, my prospects are good, and
society offers me every inducement to be happy.
You, dear Hagar—I can read it all between the
lines of your brief letters—you are lonely and
friendless. You have borne stings and insults, sorrows
and disappointments, and you are, but for your
indomitable spirit, almost breaking down under it.
Is this fair? Will you prolong the struggle and inflict
continuous pain on me as well as yourself?

You know I will not intrude upon you without
your permission and I will not urge my own longing
and love or even natural and intense desire I feel to
see the child you have borne. But I must mention
his right to a father's love and care—his probable
hard future without it.

Oh, my loved one! for one moment let my heart
speak to yours. Let my great love plead for us both. I
want you, I long to fold you in my arms and lift you
with me to a realm of pure happiness. You will not

torture me longer—call me to your side, sweet one,

with your next word to me.

PAUL

Overcome with the glowing burden of his words and the pleadings of her own heart Hagar sat alone, weak, trembling, longing, for hours. And still she could not bring herself to write the short sentence that would bring him swiftly to her side, "Come to me."

XXII

Creatures of Our Environments

While Hagar was still hesitating, her whole being in a throbbing, passionate tumult, her love for Paul struggling bravely against a life-long resolve, her baby boy, for the first time in his short, sweet existence, showed symptoms of illness. She resorted to some simple remedy of her own, took every hygienic measure possible, and gave him untiring care and attention; but it was all in vain. He grew worse and nothing she could do seemed to have any effect. Esther, pale and anxious as the mother, first whispered the dread word "scarlet fever," for she knew it was in the neighborhood. Somehow, she could not say when or in what way, little Paul had caught the disease in one of his daily airings.

Some one may have had it lurking about them, and stopped to admire him, as many did, though Hagar never allowed strangers to kiss the child. At any rate the fever grew higher and Hagar very anxious sent for a good physician. She was too strong and self-contained to become frightened even when the doctor gravely shook his head over the little sufferer, but every motherly instinct flew to the rescue, every nerve became intense and strained—in that condition she could have fought with death for days and nights sleeplessly and scarcely felt the ordeal.

An hour came when the man of physic said there was no hope. Hagar's face grew more rigid and white but not for one moment did she believe him. "I will not let my baby die," she said firmly. "I will hold him here by my love and my determination."

Then she thought of Paul. "He must see his boy. He can help me to keep him."

And all her heart went out to him in longing. How he could sustain her! How inexpressibly dear his presence would be to her now in this hour of trouble! And without further thought as to what would come afterward—what their future relations might be, she had the message flashed over the wires that should call him to her side and that of their sick child.

The baby did not die. It seemed that by sheer force of her will she kept the little life fluttering there until nature could rally after the shock of the attack of the disease.

Two days passed after word was sent, and Hagar leaned over the baby boy, trembling with joy that the white skin was once more cool and moist, the breath even, and the delicate little form once again quiet and full of repose.

Some one came softly, gently to her side. A voice rich with feeling murmured her name. Hagar looked up and saw Paul—bronzed and bearded, but so strong, so loving, so completely *all* that she had missed in her lonely life, that one long sigh of relief was her only welcome as she fell in his arms, fainting for the first time in her life.

But this was only for a moment and would not have happened at all had she not been worn with watching and anxiety. Very soon she opened her eyes and looked into those tender blue ones beaming with gladness, and wondered to herself how she could ever have sent him away. And yet—was that not what she was to do again?

Together they bent over the motionless, wax like form of their child; he was out of danger, but had not yet given a conscious look or an intelligible sound.

"How beautiful he is!" said Paul, gazing earnestly on the softly curved features and then on Hagar's face, as if to trace a likeness.

"He is like you, Paul. Only I think his eyes resemble mine."

Just then the child turned his head and opened his eyes disclosing the dark, slumbrous depths of his mother's eyes without their strange, unreadable sadness. The little child had never heard the word "papa" and he was not at all familiar with the faces of men. Yet his first conscious effort on awakening and seeing the handsome, loving, manly face bending over him was to smile brightly and reach his weak little hands toward him.

Great tears came into the strong man's eyes; he stooped and gathered the little one, so gently, so lovingly in his arms—it was like a mother's caress.

"I can never leave him now, Hagar."

And Hagar looked on and smiled.

A little later, one moonlit evening, the two sat together, the moonlight streaming in through the long windows, resting like a benediction on their heads. There was no other light in the room and a gentle breeze redolent of fall flowers and fading leaves floated in through the open window. The street outside was quiet, only a low musical whistle of some musing boy leaning over a gate perhaps, and the occasional whir of carriage wheels on the smooth pavement, breaking the stillness. They had been conversing in low tones for some time, but now a silence had fallen between them that did not correspond with their full hearts. Paul was the first to speak.

"Dear Hagar, you almost make me believe you are fanatical—as badly prejudiced in one extreme as most people are in the other. Bring your calm, cool judgment to bear upon this question as though it were a matter apart from ourselves, and you will see that I am right. I acknowledge every argument against the institution of marriage as entrenched in church and state, and yet—because of these arguments would you doom people to lives of loneliness, lovelessness, celibacy?"

"It is not that, Paul. I do not ignore the social and sexual natures of human beings. I do not expect people to give up love and domestic happiness. But I do say that people are all wrong *now;* there is so much sadness, suffering and misery in the world; so many hopes blighted, so many rosy dreams turned to darkness, so many tender loves changed into hatred and bitterness. No one knows what the right relations of men and women are. I mean by "right" the relations which will bring the highest and best happiness to the race and to individuals. It never can be found until they are both *free*—until all the old conventional shackles have been shaken off. A free womankind will discover what is best for her, for her children, for her lover. But in the meantime, some one must be pioneer. Some one must teach people that there is a slavery—that it is this slavery which causes so much suffering. So accustomed to bondage has the race become in centuries of oppression, that they have come to believe it a normal state and have no conception of a condition of liberty; as the eyeless fish

of dark caves, can not conceive of light, and could not be made

to believe in it, so they are blind to the glorious possibilities of

boundless, shining freedom. It is not enough to say that were we

economically free the rest would follow—progress toward perfect

freedom must move in a broad, universal march. While one half

the race are in a willing servitude the whole onward movement

must be retarded.

"I have startled and shocked the little world in which I

am known; from now on they could be made to *think*. I ought

to go on alone. I should show them that a woman may be an

individual—a self-supporting, self-reliant useful and happy

woman without taking upon herself marriage bonds, even though

she claim her right to become a mother."

"My dear, you cannot show them an impossibility. You may

teach the people by words and actions that the old customs and

beliefs are wrong; but the example you wish to place before them

would be an effort to show them that men and women do not

need each other, and that is not what you wish to do, and is not

the lesson that human beings will ever learn."

"No, no, Paul, most assuredly it is not. I do not wish to set

such a lesson. I do not wish to be inconsistent—I—I do not seem

to see the light as clearly as I always have."

"That is because you are trying to do an unnatural thing. We love each other, yet you would that each should walk his way alone. Hagar, my loved one," and Paul leaned forward and placed his hand over hers, as it lay on her lap, speaking earnestly and solemnly, "I must submit to your decision if, after due consideration, you make sure it comes from the depths of your soul. But I cannot, cannot leave you and little Paul. You cannot let me go; it is such a useless, cruel sacrifice. Why do you insist upon it?"

Hagar bowed her head upon their folded hands for some moments in silence. There were tears glittering upon them when she again looked up,—the last tribute to a resolution which had grown up with her—was part of her being.

"You are right, Paul. I cannot give you up."

He was about to clasp her in his arms, but she drew back.

"I do not mean marriage, Paul. That ends, at best, in indifference, commonplaceness, weariness of spirit and I could not endure that. Live near us. Be within reach when I need your presence, your advice, your encouragement."

"No, Hagar, I cannot consent to that. Your experience must have taught you that in such an arrangement, *you* must suffer. Until society has reformed sufficiently to give free and independent women an equal chance for life and happiness with men, it is the duty and delight of a true man to throw round the woman he loves all the safeguards and protection in his power. Not in that limited sense now understood by those words, which makes a protected woman also a subservient one, but in the sense of seeking true equality. Since society places woman at such disadvantage, men, as individuals, must make that disadvantage good. Marry me, dear Hagar, and only such part of that ceremony as makes your lot easier in life will ever be recognized by me. You shall belong to yourself body and mind; I shall have no 'rights' over you except to love and care for you."

Hagar gave him a kiss, with her lustrous eyes full of tenderness, but ah! in their depths that old, sad, solemn look which had been so marked in childhood and girlhood, came back and dwelt beneath the gentle radiance.

XXIII

Conclusion

"Does happiness never endure? Does love never last? Are only the dead lovers the true ones? For, in romance and story, the truest lovers have died young. The old have no tales of love told of them. It is sad to think that it is so; that not far in the future, Paul, you and I will be humdrum old people, nagging at each other, perhaps, and wishing secretly in our hearts that we were free. I wish the end of the world would come before that time."

"Love, be happy *now*. Do not borrow sorrow from a possible future. I cannot imagine such a fate for you and me. As long as you are what you are now I must love you. I can but try with all the powers of my being to make myself worthy of you, and trust that you will love me to the end."

"But we will not always be what we are today, Paul. The way before us is misty and dark. I wish we could find the right path—a pathway that would always lie in the sunshine."

Hagar looked up wistfully as she spoke and drew her hand from the waters rippling at the boat's prow. They had gone to the country where the cool, fresh breezes were fast building up little Paul's strength and health. Today they were out on a smooth, slow river with drooping willows shading the still waters, and a warm golden haze resting over the quiet scene; Paul rested on his oars and Hagar reclined on the broad seat in the stern of the boat, little Paul lay asleep on a bed of cushions between them.

"Hagar, let us *try*—let us try as never lovers did before. It is only through the right understanding of ourselves, of the little claim which any outside power has over us, of the beauties of liberty and individuality that we can find happiness. The ceremony pronounced by a third party has little to do with it, whether omitted or not. There have been couples who have come together, dispensing with the officiousness of church and state, believing that the legality of the union was what made the usual trouble; yet their unions have almost invariably ended in sorrow, passion, disappointment, bitterness, disgrace. It is because they entered upon their relations with the same old feelings, the same old ignorance, the same old spirit of exaction, exclusiveness, ownership, jealousy, which is the inherent part of the old marriage institution. All they got rid of was the mere form of the marriage ceremony.

"Now for ourselves: we have what so many have not—the means of establishing a healthful, happy home. A home in the true sense of the word cannot be made within four small, meager walls, where poverty must also dwell, the man becoming stolid and imbruted at hard work, the woman being tied down to a round of petty, worrying duties. Even the best of isolated homes, we may find in the future, are not conductive to the highest happiness; it is impossible to fortell what wise co-operation may yet accomplish. But in the meantime, *our* home will be our own, and we must bring our best judgment to bear upon it. In my opinion, it should be roomy, airy, and light, and furnished with a view to comfort, and pleasure to the senses. We must each have our own apartments as well as parlor; reading room, dining room and kitchen in common. The privacy of each shall be as greatly respected as though we were mere acquaintances. I must strive, dear, never to be exact or demand or command, or reproach you, so long as you live up to your own highest ideals. I need not say you never will be exacting or fault finding, because I know your nature. We will not rashly fan our love to white flames of passion only to be consumed, and in time find our lives dead ashes around us. And as far as I can make you, Hagar, you shall be free as the zephyrs that are playing with your hair at this moment."

"But, Paul," Hagar said softly, "supposing in our feeling of freedom, one of us should sometime love another. Will not the other grieve and die?"

"We do not know what may happen—we cannot pledge ourselves. Vows should not avert such a fate, if it is to come to us. It does not seem possible now. I hope we may both enjoy many sweet friendships, even loves; yet I believe, I hope, that between us will be such complete congeniality, such perfect understanding, such close sympathy and ready response, that no one else ever *can* be to either what we are to each other. Between people who are equally strong in character, in power to love, in self-reliance, who are independent financially and socially, there is much more likelihood of a mutual love that is lasting than if one is clinging and dependent, the other masterful and strong. Ours shall be a new experiment; we will *see* if under the best conditions possible in the world at present, love *is* lasting and exclusive. Ah, Hagar! I have loved you and you only, since you were a little child. I am loving you more every day I live. Is it likely I shall grow weary of much loving?"

Hagar's face was bright with hope and tenderness; but she had no word to say. The sun, low in the west, sent one last golden ray radiating like a blessing over the light brown curls and the jetty tresses of the two, then the softness and silence of a warm, early autumn evening fell upon them.

————————

One day when the ideal home was nearly completed, Hagar had an unlooked-for visitor. Going into the parlor with the expectation of seeing some ambitious agent, she was confronted by her brother-in-law, Dan. He was older looking and there were careworn lines about the face, but she knew him instantly. She had not believed she could be so glad to see a man she had never liked, but he brought up such clear memories of Lucy, of her other brothers and sisters, of her mother, of the humble little brown cottage where all her girlhood had been passed, that, sad as they were, she clasped Dan's hand with both her own, and smiled, and exclaimed, and laughed again, with tears in her bright eyes, for greeting. She had written to Lucy once since she lived in her present home, but had received no answer; indeed not one from her old home had deigned to notice her since her child was born. Still she could never forget them entirely, or cherish harsh feelings toward them.

"I am so glad to see you, Dan; now sit down and tell me how you and Lucy are getting along, how you came to find me, how every body is that I used to know."

"Well, I don't rightly know how to commence," said Dan awkwardly, for he was not accustomed to tasteful parlors, and this elegant and handsome woman did not seem like the Hagar of old whom he used to hold in some contempt for her insignificant looks and queer ways.

"I had to come to the city—well, at least I thought I had to, and as I knew your address I thought I'd call on you. Lucy—she ain't very well—I know she'd give her eyes to see you, though she don't say much about it. Both the oldest boys, your brothers, have gone out west—herdin' cows I believe. The next girl has left home, workin' somewhere in a milliner store. The rest of 'em are running wild. Your step-mother is a big, fat, lazy woman with just git up enough about her to bully the old man; he's grown awfully old and bent—seems dreadfully unhappy an' miserable, don't do much of anything outside o' work hours but read the bible and groan. Well, let's see—who else do you want to know about?"

"I want to know more about Lucy—everything in fact. Have you more children? Are you both happier than you used to be?"

Dan heaved a sigh that was half groan—half imprecation. "Happy! Well, the less said about that the better. We've had two more children since you left and one of 'em died; it's the best off of the lot."

"What is the matter with you and Lucy?"

"I'll be d———switched, if I know. Mebbe it's my fault. But many and many a time, I've thought it over and resolved to be jus' as good to her as I knew how, but that aggravatin', naggin' way o' hers beats me every time; then I'm a brute. Some how spite of all the troubles we've had, I'm that tied to that woman I can't bear to stay away from her—I can't bear to think o' her with any body else. I wish we could get along peaceably, but instead of that it's fusses and quarrels, and repinin's and scolding of her part till—well, I got desperate and, the fact is, I've left. I just fixed 'em up the best I could, and come away. I'm going to send 'em money when I can earn it, and be a wanderin' vagabond, hungerin' fer home and children, the rest of my life."

Hagar looked at Dan in sad surprise. He was the picture of dejection and hopelessness; rough and half barbarian as he had always seemed to her, he was not a bad man at heart, and she knew he was not the kind of person to succeed at anything without the encouragement and inspiration of home and creatures dependent upon him. He would drift about like a rudderless boat and land broken and ruined where the world threw up its other wretched driftwood. He was more ignorant than bad, but with the circumstances against him he might soon become anything that was miserable and degraded. Lucy was not fit to live alone with three children; she was only a creature of impulse, ignorant, untrained, undeveloped, crushed out of the semblance of what she might have been had the conditions of her life been better. Hagar wondered if she *could* do them any good at this late day.

"Dan," she said sympathetically, "I am sorry for you both. I wish I could help you. Perhaps you expect me, with my ideas of personal freedom, to advise you to remain apart. But I believe if more people understood the laws of equal freedom, it would unite and preserve families, loves, and affections, rather than destroy them. Everything worth saving would be saved. I know that you will be wretched away from Lucy and your children. I know she will be helpless, lonely, unwise, unhappy without you. Neither of you have any prospect of better, wiser or happier lives apart than you have together; if you had, I would not advise you to go back. But I do now. But in going back I want to ask you to decide on a different course entirely, from any you have ever pursued. If you were staying away, you would not be scolding, interfering with Lucy's wishes, intruding your presence upon her at all times, whether welcome or not. Now, though you go back for the sake of expediency, treat her just this way. Make yourself as comfortable a room as you can over your stables and leave the house, except at meal-times and when invited, to Lucy and the children. Treat her as though she were a lady upon whom you had no claims whatever, but whom you wish to please and attract. Do for her every little kindness in your power, but above everything else don't obtrude yourself; don't exact or demand. If she wants to go out with the young people arrange it so she can go, and be glad she is happy. Don't find fault with anything she does. I will write to Lucy and give her also some good advice. Depend upon it, if you heed it, I will come and see you next year, and find you a pair of bright-faced, happy lovers!"

"Why, that would be the same as a separation! We would not *be* husband and wife if we lived that way."

"Well, then forget you are husband and wife, if those words carry with them such import. You were never happy in those relations—try now you will be as two individuals without any claims upon each other except those that are spontaneous and natural. You both love your children and your home; you each have a right to the home and the society of the children; now if you cease to make demands, to claim unwillingly-given privileges, you *can* exercise these rights in peace; and I haven't any doubt in the world it will lead to happiness."

"It's a strange notion—livin' that way. I don't know as I could carry it out. I can't keep away from Lucy and I'm afraid I'd half kill the first man I saw talkin' to her."

"You must try, Dan. You know how miserable you have been—you know how wretched you will be, if you remain away from home altogether. Isn't the other plan a better one? Lucy may like the society of other men—that is only natural—but when she sees she need never fear you, and that she can only have your love

by inviting or attracting it, she will soon learn to care more for
you than any else. Stay away long enough, Dan, to think this over
seriously and resolve upon it, then go home and *try* sincerely and
earnestly."

"I vow I believe I'll take your advice. I don't see any other
outcome. You've given me some hope, anyway, for I ain't ashamed
to say I was about the miserablest man in the city when I came in
here. Say, now will you come down and see us next year? I own
I've been set against you and set Lucy up not to write to you,
(though she didn't need much settin' up) but I'm getting over
those old notions, and by the look of you I know you must have
had some good reason for what you did. I hope you'll forgive me
an' come and bring—bring your family."

So saying, he arose to go, his awkwardness lost in the new
thoughts awakened within him, and offered his hand to say good
bye. Hagar gave him a few more parting words as she held the
big, rough hand, and experienced a more kindly feeling for the
impulsive, undisciplined man than she ever had in her life. Her
old love for Lucy rushed back again, and she almost prayed for
her future happiness as Dan went down the steps and slowly out
of her sight.

They are all living yet, gentle reader—for gentle you
must be if you are reading—and it is not yet long enough past
the events related, to determine whether Hagar and Paul have

solved the problem or not. They are faithful workers in the great struggles of society toward freedom and justice; they have learned to come close to the hearts of the people and they love their work as they are loved by those who have suffered; persecution and misrepresentation of course they meet, and expect it. But this does not deter them, for they could not be silent if they would.

All society is heaving, struggling, feeling the throes of pain for the birth of a new idea. As yet, but the suffering, the tumult, the apparent chaos which comes with a great change—the clash and danger and sacrifice wherever progress moves onward over an old corrupt, deeply-embedded wrong, the seeming confusion, and agony in the breaking up of old customs that have festered and grown into the vital parts of humanity—all these, as yet, are what we *see*, rather than the promise of a sweet, wise, peaceful delight that is to come in the future.

The woman is on her knees now and her struggles *hurt*. When once she is risen and shall stand side by side with man, they will both look toward the rising sun of liberty and be bathed wholly in its light and warmth.

Finis

Appendix A

Shadows

March 17th 1893 (appeared on the front page of *Lucifer* next to Chapter 1 of *Hagar Lyndon*).

In a low log hut, standing under the shadow of a huge and jagged mountain, a woman sat with a little child in her arms. Her soft voice floated out on the light quivering air in a lullaby song, a plaintiveness in it sadder and more helpless than the wail of the child she would hush. A mighty solitude rested on all about— not such silence as visits the plains—but an awesome hush—the eternal watch of the grand old peaks, under the blue, majestic dome. A flaming sky behind the western hills, a purple haze to the south, a lavish waving of fleecy white veiling around the heads of the mountains toward the north, framed in the little world this woman looked upon. No human being beside herself and child was within it. Sometimes when the shadows were heavier, a man would come wearily up the path from the valley below, and night would close round the lonely but "sacred" little home.

But while she sits there, a picture forms on the sky before her, in it she sees herself amid a throng of laughing young companions, the brightest and merriest among them. She hears the music of the olden time, smells the perfumes of roses, feels the genial spirit of the well filled home. She thrills again with the hopes and dreams of a busy, famous future, knows the sweetness in action, energy, free life. Ah! then love had come, and how happy she had been! How dear it seemed to her! For the sake of one dear being, she had thrown all else to the winds. She would follow him to the ends of the earth—and she had. She became all-in-all to him, and he to her.

He had not failed her, he had not deceived her. Yet how unspeakably sad were the dark dreamy eyes tonight! What pathos in the trembling voice, what longing and loneliness in the pale young face! Something of her had never been given to love. It tugged at her soul and wore her out with its struggles. Is it possible to give one's self entirely to the keeping of another?

—*May Huntley*

Shadows.

In a low log hut, standing under the shadow of a huge and jagged mountain, a woman sat with a little child in her arms. Her soft voice floated out on the light quivering air in a lullaby song, a plaintiveness in it sadder and more helpless than the wail of the child she would hush. A mighty solitude rested on all about—not such silence as visits the plains—but an awesome hush—the eternal watch of the grand old peaks, under the blue, majestic dome. A flaming sky behind the western hills, a purple haze to the south, a lavish waving of fleecy white veiling around the heads of the mountains toward the north, framed in the little world this woman looked upon. No human being beside herself and child was within it. Sometime when the shadows were heavier, a man would come wearily up the path from the valley below, and night would close round the lonely but "sacred" little home.

But while she sits there, a picture forms on the sky before her, in it she sees herself amid a throng of laughing young companions, the brightest and merriest among them. She hears the music of the olden time, smells the perfumes of roses, feels the genial spirit of the well filled home. She thrills again with the hopes and dreams of a busy, famous future, knows the sweetness in action, energy, free life. Ah! then love had come, and how happy she had been! How dear it seemed to her! For the sake of one dear being, she had thrown all else to the winds. She would follow him to the ends of the earth—and she had. She became all-in-all to him, and he to her.

He had not failed her, he had not deceived her. Yet how unspeakably sad were the dark dreamy eyes tonight! What pathos in the trembling voice, what longing and loneliness in the pale young face! Something of her had never been given to love. It tugged at her soul and wore her out with its struggles. Is it possible to give one's self entirely to the keeping of another?

MAY HUNTLEY.

May Huntley (Lizzie M. Holmes), "Shadows" (*Lucifer the Light-Bearer*, March 17, 1893).

Appendix B

Honor to Whom Honor Is Due

From *Lucifer*, July 14, 1893.

———————

Hail to brave and good Governor Altgeld! He has not only opened the prison doors that wrongfully closed upon three men nearly six years ago, but he has given to the world in clear, forcible terms his reasons for doing so righteous an act. Not as an act of mercy, he declares, for if these men were guilty of murder they deserve no pardon, but because they never ought to have been sent there in the first place. He cares not that his reasons disclose the wickedness of prosecuting attorney, bailiff, judge and jury—but gives the *truth*, with the proofs held in his hand! The whole world will know now, what a handful of devoted friends have been trying to get before the public ever since that fatal 11th of November, 1887.

Alas! in rejoicing at the liberation of these innocent men, we cannot shut out the memory of those five graves at Waldheim, where a monument to the martyrs lying there, was but yesterday unveiled. Every reason which the Governor so clearly set forth, why the three men should never have been incarcerated, tells with equal force against that awful act that consigned these men to that spot. Governor Altgeld's kindly hand cannot reach them, but his words will help to clear their names of the obloquy, misrepresentation and abuse which have been heaped upon them.

We rejoice in this tardy act of justice; we congratulate Fielden, Schwab and Neebe and all their loving friends, and we heartily thank the Governor of Illinois.

—Lizzie M. Holmes

For Lucifer.

Honor to Whom Honor is Due.

Hail to brave and good Governor Altgeld! He has not only opened the prison doors that wrongfully closed upon three men nearly six years ago, but he has given to the world in clear, forcible terms his reasons for doing so righteous an act. Not as an act of mercy, he declares, for if these men were guilty of murder they deserve no pardon, but because they never ought to have been sent there in the first place. He cares not that his reasons disclose the wickedness of prosecuting attorney, bailiff, judge and jury—but gives the *truth*, with the proofs held in his hand! The whole world will know now, what a handful of devoted friends have been trying to get before the public ever since that fatal 11th of November, 1887.

Alas! in rejoicing at the liberation of these innocent men, we cannot shut out the memory of those five graves at Waldheim, where a monument to the martyrs lying there, was but yesterday unveiled. Every reason which the Governor so clearly set forth, why the three men should never have been incarcerated, tells with equal force against that awful act that consigned these men to that spot. Governor Altgeld's kindly hand cannot reach them, but his words will help to clear their names of the obloquy, misrepresentation and abuse which have been heaped upon them.

We rejoice in this tardy act of justice; we congratulate Fielden, Schwab and Neebe and all their loving friends, and we heartily thank the Governor of Illinois.   LIZZIE M. HOLMES.

Lizzie M. Holmes, "Honor to Whom Honor Is Due" (*Lucifer the Light-Bearer*, July 14, 1893).

Appendix C

Symposium on the Story

From *Lucifer*, June 23, 1893.

A break in the story this week. The authoress writes us that she has been "moving," and that she has been caring for her sick daughter and infant grandchild, and altogether has not been able to revise the manuscript story as she desires to do before sending. This explanation we think should be satisfactory to the many readers of LUCIFER who anxiously look for the weekly installment of the story and wish it were longer. Taking advantage of the temporary break and to satisfy a not unreasonable desire for some expression of opinion in regard to the merits or demerits of the serial we herewith publish, and partly republish, a few sample extracts from letters that have from time to time been sent us— letters that were not designed for publication but yet were not marked "private and confidential." The objections have without exception come from the masculine side of the house, while the demand for back numbers to the "beginning of the story" has at length practically exhausted our reserves of certain issues.

— Ed. L.

I presume I am in the minority, but I cannot but feel that the tone of LUCIFER is lowered by the publication of such stories as Hagar Lyndon. I read three or four chapters, but could not get interested. In fact, I do not think that LUCIFER is large enough to have any space to spare for stories, no matter how much of a moral the author may desire to teach. Enclosed please find small contribution.

> — *J.C. Steinmetz*
> *Devon, Pa., 5 23-'93*

I failed to receive No. 480 of LUCIFER. Please send me the missing No. as I do not want to lose any of the story.

> —*Nell Pepper*
> *Ottumwa, Iowa, 6-13-'93*

My paper of June 2d has failed to reach me, up to date. I am very sorry to miss a number as we are all deeply interested in the continued story of Hagar Lyndon, also the many other items of interest in your paper. There [are] a number of my neighbors very much pleased with LUCIFER. I trust you will hear from some of them ere long.

Most sincerely a co-worker,

> —*Mrs. M. E. Dobson*

I failed to get No. 26 of Lucifer and as I am interested in Hagar

Lyndon, would like for you to please send me that number.

—*Clara Reed*
Loami, Ill., 6-16-'93

For some unknown reason I have never got No's 475 and 478 of

Lucifer. As I am much interested in the story, Hagar Lyndon,

I don't like to miss any of the No's. Will you be so kind as to

replace the missing papers, and oblige.

—*Mary C. Parker*
Pine Island, Minn., 6-12-'93

Mr. Moses Harman—Dear Sir: Enclosed you will find 25

cents. Please send me Lucifer for three months, and your back

numbers, beginning of the story, Hagar Lyndon. I am perfectly

carried away with your paper. Don't fail to send me the back

numbers. I just think it is the greatest paper that is out.

—*Mrs. J. D. Dryburge*
Halifax, Virginia.

Hagar Lyndon's life is nearly a reproduction of my own childhood

and girlhood (if I ever had such a thing). In Mr. Lyndon I saw my

father with the religious element left out. Otherwise the portrait

is complete. In Mrs. Lyndon my own crushed mother, and in

Lucy and Dan my only sister and her husband.

No, the story is not overdrawn. The half even has not been told. It cannot be told by tongue or pen. It is only those who have been unfortunate enough to live under such conditions that can realize how true it is, and such "homes" as that are not rare by any means. I know plenty of them.

— Mrs. E. M. S——
Stockton, Calif., 6-9-'93.

Enclosed please find my check for $50. Please send Lucifer one year beginning with the first "Hagar Lyndon" number of March 17th, to each of the enclosed list of thirty-three. Perhaps some good may grow therefrom. It might be well to *mark* in blue or red the first copies of the "Hagar Lyndon" numbers.

Very Truly,

— S. A. C——

It has been said of the Markland letter, "It is exaggerated[,] an extreme case," etc. I once asked a respectable conservative physician if he had ever known a case like the one related in the Markland letter? He said, "Yes, plenty of them."

What is to hinder "plenty of them?" There is no law either human or divine to prevent such cases. The man who thus outrages his wife may be thoroughly respectable, an honored member of society and pillar of the church. In the story of Hagar, Deacon Lyndon and his wife, especially the submissive obedience of the latter, has been termed "exaggerated," when they are in reality a model pair, fulfilling all the requirements—she obeying her husband, "in sorrow bringing forth children," he "ruling over her" in compliance with the code accepted by a large majority of members of our christian civilization. Do christians call a character "exaggerated" for a too strict obedience to laws they profess to believe are divine? If all men enforced all the obedience the law allows or requires, exaggerated cases would be far more frequent than now. That they are not considered criminal is proven by the fact that not the perpetrator but the witness who testifies is punished.

— ETNA

"Our war celebrations are a legacy to punish us for rapine and murder. In mouth it is sweet as honey, in the belly bitter as wormwood, but material man knows it not."

A Symposium on *Hagar Lyndon* (*Lucifer the Light-Bearer*, June 23, 1893).

Hagar Lyndon's life is nearly a reproduction of my own childhood and girlhood (if I ever had such a thing.) In Mr. Lyndon I saw my father with the religious element left out. Otherwise the portrait is complete. In Mrs. Lyndon my own crushed mother, and in Lucy and Dan my only sister and her husband.

No, the story is not overdrawn. The half even has not been told. It cannot be told by tongue or pen. It is only those who have been unfortunate enough to live under such conditions that can realize how true it is, and such "homes" as that are not rare by any means. I know plenty of them.

STOCKTON, CALIF., 6-9-'93.   MRS. E. M. S——.

Enclosed please find my check for $50. Please send LUCIFER one year beginning with the first "Hagar Lyndon" number of March 17th, to each of the enclosed list of thirty-three. Perhaps some good may grow therefrom. It might be well to *mark* in blue or red the first copies of the "Hagar Lyndon" numbers.   Very Truly,   S. A. C——.

It has been said of the Markland letter, "It is exaggerated an extreme case," etc. I once asked a respectable conservative physician if he had ever known a case like the one related in the Markland letter? He said, "Yes, plenty of them."

What is to hinder "plenty of them?" There is no law either human or divine to prevent such cases. The man who thus outrages his wife may be thoroughly respectable, an honored member of society and pillar of the church. In the story of Hagar, Deacon Lyndon and his wife, especially the submissive obedience of the latter, has been termed "exaggerated," when they are in reality a model pair, fulfilling all the requirements—she obeying her husband, "in sorrow bringing forth children," he "ruling over her" in compliance with the code accepted by a large majority of members of our christian civilization. Do christians call a character "exaggerated" for a too strict obedience to laws they profess to believe are divine? If all men enforced all the obedience the law allows or requires, exaggerated cases would be far more frequent than now. That they are not considered criminal is proven by the fact that not the perpetrator but the witness who testifies is punished.   ETNA.

"Our war celebrations are a legacy to punish us for rapine and murder. In the mouth it is sweet as honey, in the belly bitter as wormwood, but material man knows it not."

A Symposium on *Hagar Lyndon*, continued (*Lucifer the Light-Bearer*, June 23, 1893).

About the Author

Lizzie May (Hunt) Swank Holmes (1850–1926) was an anarchist, labor organizer, and writer. Born in Ohio, she worked as a school teacher and often taught music. After the death of her first husband, Holmes moved herself and her children to Chicago, where she became involved in the labor movement, working for the Women's Assembly No. 1798 of the Knights of Labor in 1881 and then eventually joining the Chicago branch of the International Working People's Association (IWPA). Holmes was the assistant editor of the Chicago-based *The Alarm*, which was one of several radical socialist and anarchist papers in Chicago in the 1880s, and she was friends with many of the so-called Haymarket Martyrs, including Albert Parsons, the editor of *The Alarm*. Parsons, along with several other radical men, was tried and hung for his purported involvement in a bomb blast that killed police and protesters during a labor demonstration for the eight-hour work day in Haymarket Square in 1886. Most of Holmes's known work comes from periodicals, including *The Alarm*, *Lucifer the Light-Bearer*, and *Free Society*. Just before the turn of the century, Holmes and her second husband left Chicago to settle in Colorado, and, finally, New Mexico, where she died in 1926.